Boomtown 1880

Justice

V.K. Lares

Dedication

This book and all that follow are dedicated to the memory of my dearest friend Jason, whose wisdom taught me so many lessons about life from which I still continue to learn from.

I miss you my friend.

Chapter 1

The Western half of the New Mexico Territory, Spring 1853

Come along boy. Time for bed." William's father Jacob called to his ten-year-old son from the inner circle of the wagon train as William sat outside the perimeter gazing at the stars and believing in his parent's dream of a better life west of the Mississippi. After supper and evening chores, the boy spent his tired evenings chucking dirt clods, rocks and whatever he found at his feet into the night sky. The moon's silver crescent gleamed as a target for his imagination. His thin, mighty arm tossed each pebble as though he were mighty David and the moon was Goliath. He held his breath listening and counting the seconds it took for the thump of the rocks and lumps of dirt to hit the desert floor.

Behind him, nearly drowning out the sound of the impacts, his parents and fellow wagon train pioneers celebrated having reached ever closer to their destination and those friends made during the long travel west parted their respective ways to set up homesteads. The harmonicas and other homemade instruments provided the music that rang cheerily in the background. Weeks on end the words "San Francisco, California, and gold" were repeated during the arduous trip from Louisiana. Would this journey ever end? He was tired. Hungry half the time. Always dirty. Not that being dirty mattered that much to a boy his age, but swimming in a creek now and again like the one he had back home would have been fun.

They could have done without the school marm who joined the expedition in Texas to find a new life west. However, even William had to admit Miss Harceface kept his and the other children's days busy enough with her lessons and ciphering did keep their minds off the day's trail dust they regularly spat. Arithmetic and Billy Jenkins 'ability to make him laugh by calling the teacher Miss Horseface behind her back kept his spirits high. He did not want to be disrespectful, but her face kind of did look like a horse and he quietly smiled whenever he was called upon to answer, correctly, a question.

The group had been traveling for what seemed a thousand years to young William and they still hadn't even crossed the border into California. He was beginning to think the promise of a new life and a real bed would never come to pass. The promise land was just talk and something that Pa and uncle Frank had made up. A fairy tale told to him and Ma.

Fueled by the fever of gold, the decision made, William's family joined the wagon train and headed west to capture the riches of what others had already found in the hills of California.

"William! I won't tell you again!" Jacob broke William's reverie.

William snapped his head toward the wagons and people now settling for the night. "Coming Pa." Snatching a last clump of dirt, drew back his arm taking proper aim to let it sail until it hit the moon, and froze. He gazed as something crossed the moon's path and descended slowly through the scattered clouds. The round-shaped looking glass reflected the starlight, distorting the moon's image. Though distant, its size compared to that of two fingers width at the end of an outstretched arm. The object floated to the ground, disappearing from William's view.

Eyes wide, William let out the breath he had not known he held, dropped the last clod he meant to throw, turned and dashed to the family wagon where his father stood handing tin plates to his wife. Breathless, Will slid the last three feet to a halt throwing dust into the air spraying the clean dishes his mother was packing, readying for the next day's travel. "William! For pity sake!"

William ignoring his mother's chastise turned excitedly to his father, "Pa. Pa! You gotta see this!" Will tugged anxiously at his father's jacket.

"Will! What on earth..."

"Come now Pa, before it goes away. It's a floating looking glass right in front of the moon! I swear, Pa!"

William had a firm grasp on his father's jacket, tugging him away from his mother, the crowd and the wagons. Jacob grabbed his rifle that leaned against the wagon's tailgate and hurried to the site of William's concern.

"What are we looking at Will?" Remaining calm, Jacob quietly reached for the powder flask at his side, holding his cap and ball rifle across his mid section readying to load for potential danger.

"Pa, it was right up there in the sky. It drifted in front of the moon and fell to the ground near those hills yonder!" William pointed in the direction of the object of his excitement.

"What the devil are you talking about, son? What floated? What drifted?"

"The looking glass, Pa. Right there," Will said again pointing toward the distant mountains.

Jacob dropped his rifle butt onto his boot and rested his arms across the barrel end. He spoke with concern, but was not condescending. "Now, Will. You and I both know a looking glass cannot float and certainly not across the moon. The night sky in these unknown parts of the desert can play tricks on a man. Sometimes we see something and it turns out to be something else. Remember when you thought your Uncle Frank was a ghost and it turned out that Frank sampled too much of that moonshine and fell into the flour barrel?"

"Yeah, but Pa this is different."

"Okay, son. I believe that you saw something. Whatever it was it's gone now. Time to get to bed. We got a long day tomorrow. It'll all get sorted out, I'm sure. Now, run along and don't go scaring your sister and your Ma." Jacob smiled gently, touched Will's shoulder to turn him toward the wagons and gave a gentle swat on his hind to lovingly urge him to bed. Jacob also tugged on his powder flask and expected to sleep lightly that night with the rifle at his side believing his son saw something. He hoped it was a bear and not Indians.

"But, Pa I swear I saw..."

"I believe you, son," Jacob said cutting off William's persistence. "Now git."

William looked into his father's expression of kindness, nodded and obeyed. Jacob watched Will scuff his way back to the wagon, then turned to the mountains and moon for a last watchful look wondering what his son might have seen in the night sky that excited eldest child to such a degree of concern.

Whether Jacob believed William or not, William was assured that his father respected his word and having been taught never to lie, was proud that his father trusted that word enough to not question its validity.

The next morning the wagon train continued west. William and his father never again discussed the incident of the floating looking glass.

Nine years later, in 1862, William, Jacob and his Uncle Frank traveled back to Virginia, and joined the Confederacy to fight for independence. William was killed in June of 1863 at the battle of Vicksburg, Virginia.

Chapter 2

New Mexico Territory, early March 1880

The town of Albuquerque Abigail Emerson took her midday stroll along the boardwalk, anticipating the seemingly ever present patch of mud just past the telegraph office on the edge of the thoroughfare. The air was crisp and cool. The clear blue sky was empty of clouds and the breathtaking scape of Mount Sandia was always a sight to behold in the morning. Gentlemen of all ages tipped their hats with a smile to the lovely young Miss Emerson as they crossed paths. It took only a glance from her soft hazel eyes to bewitch a man's heart. Her smile alone was enough to move the heavens and to hold her graceful hand and lay kiss upon it's back was worth facing eternal damnation. This especially was the thought of one young man who produced a bouquet with perfect timing just before her, halting her stride. The flowers were held by a hand and an arm emerging from behind the telegraph office Abigail was about to pass.

"Hmmm... Daisies at this time of year?" Abigail said as she examined the flowers in detail.
"Very difficult to find." The slight twang of the familiar young man's voice came from behind the building. "I had to wrestle three wild coyotes and one overweight florist to get them."

"Austin Baker! You did not wrestle old Mister Collins!" Abigail said with a smile in her voice.

"Well, maybe not wrestle. But, I did have to pay him double for his last batch of the season." Austin Replied.

"Knowing how much he loves daisy's I'm surprised he was willing to part with them at so low a price."

"When I told him that they were for you he loosened his grip." Austin said as he emerged from behind the building and looked Abigail in the eyes.

"Did he now?" she asked playfully as she gently took the bouquet from Austin whose hat was already in his hand covering his chest. Abigail closed her eyes and held the daisy's to her nose. She opened her eyes again looking into Austin's steely blues. Abigail was again taken with Austin's face. Rugged, yet handsome with his dark blonde hair and fair complexion. As tall as her father but not as broad with a way about him that could make you forget all the stories and gossip people tell about his past. 'People 'typically meaning the ladies in town.

"Miss, you appear to be walking without escort. Might I offer my services to assist you across the treacherous thoroughfare?"

"Very well sir, you may."

Austin dawned his hat and extended his elbow for the young lady to place her hand through and the two continued around the mud and onto the next boardwalk in front of the post office. As usual, Austin ignored the disapproving glares in his direction from the passers by.

"Might I inquire if some other young man has asked you to the fandango this evening?"

"Oh, about a dozen or so have already asked me to dance with them tonight."

"A dozen you say?" Austin said unsure if it was true or not.

"But, I told them all I had already been promised to someone else, but Henry didn't take kindly to that." Abigail's voice took on a more serious tone.

"Henry Lloyd?" Austin voice dropped with predictable contempt hearing the name and turned to Abigail. "Henry Lloyd is an ornery coot whose notion of treating a woman right is in beating her only once a week!"

"Oh hush! Henry has always been nothing but respectful of me and my daddy. That's why he working at the livery now." Abigail replied.

"Your Pa gave him work?" Austin was taken aback by this new piece of unwelcome information.

"Daddy just owns the Livery, he would never work there. That's why he hires others to attend the horses. Besides, it's just work, no need to throw yourself into a conniption." Abigail's voice sounded more lke an order than a request. Austin's jaw clenched and he huffed through his nose while his gaze could not bare to see Abigail's for that moment. He turned away and fixed on the passing coach from Loomis Fargo.

"Now, now..." Abigail said as she touched her soft hand to Austin's stubbled cheek bringing his attention back to her. "...Henry Lloyd may be looking at me, but I'm not looking at him. So let's not fret about it anymore."

Austin took a moment to collect himself and agree to the gentle kiss of his beloveds 'voice. He took her arm in his once again and they continued their stroll down the boardwalk. Austin listened to Abigail relay the idle gossip from her girlfriends and their dull notions of the people in town, the talk of the new theater set to open next week and the droll events recounted from the oyster party Abigail had attended the previous night. As much as Austin was completely enamored with Abigail, he made the realization early on that he could do without the rumors of the town being the focus of many conversations.

Austin and Abigail reached the destination of Abigail's home. Despite his upbringing in the church and the teaching that money was not the way to happiness, Austin was always in awe of the house. He had never been allowed to see the inside of her pueblo style abode with it's ornate woodworking, cobblestone walkway and hand crafted decorations. It was the most exquisite home on the street being something out of a fantasy and capturing the attention of anyone who passed by. Being the daughter of a cattle rancher had every day benefits that most other people could only dream of. By the word of Abigail's father, no young man may venture within the doors of their home. His overzealous protection of his daughter led, many thought, to the reason he only hires young girls as servants in the house. The real reason had more to do with the extra services Mister Emerson would elicit in the late hours when the rest of the house was asleep.

Austin and Abigail stood at the base of the steps leading up to the front door. As they said their farewells Austin made plan to call on her at six in the evening to escort her to the dance. He leaned slowly forward with the hopes of stealing a kiss. Abigail's hand lifted to touch Austin's chin and stop his approach.
"Not here." She said pulling away. "I will see you tonight." Abigail moved up the short flight of stairs, turning back for one last smile at Austin before disappearing through the door.

Austin's heart skipped as did his feet on his way back to the church. The cold eyes of the town had no hold on him as his smile beamed in defiance of every face trying to crush it with their hateful stares. Until, of course, his path was obstructed by an ogre. Standing shades over Austin, a single brow above beady eyes sunk into a mellon supported by a tree trunk. Shoulders the width of a door frame connected to arms that made him seem more kin to an ox with a face to match. Covered head to toe with wiry hair and an oder that you could never quite tell if it came from him or the horses. Single handedly fought off twelve savages, or was it fifteen? Perhaps even twenty in defense of a wagon of women and children bound for Santa Fe. The story always seems to change every time Austin hears it. The pillar of the community himself, Henry Lloyd.

"Good day, Henry." Austin said coldly as he tried to pass Henry Lloyd who wasn't going to have it. He stepped in front of Austin glaring down the seven and a half inches that separated their height. Austin sighed to himself knowing that he couldn't to avoid it this time.

"I see yer get'n familiar with Miss Emerson again." Henry said as eloquently as ever with his born and raised confederate defiance.

"Well, it ain't against the law to walk a young lady home, and even if it was, you ain't the law."

"I may not be da law, Baker. But, I am respected in this town. It's a much better sight for a lady of standing like Abigail to be seen with me than a --"

"A what?" Austin cut him off taking a step forward and returning Henry's hateful stare.

Henry leaned forward and with breath more foul than the entrails of a pig he finished, "Like da bastard son of a filthy loose whore."

Austin didn't flinch or blink. He'd heard this one his whole life from every person in town with an axe to grind. He took one deep breath knowing what would happen even as the words came tumbling out of his mouth.

"I'd rather be that, than a lying cheat who takes the credit for someone else's good deed. And, to set the record straight, there were only three Indians and I don't recall you being anywhere around when it happened."

Henry's gaze broke for a split second. The only one who noticed was Austin as he watched Henry's beady eyes shift away for a moment to see if anyone else heard. Henry Lloyd had not been responsible for the daring rescue and never knew who was, until now. This confounded the filthy yeti enough to make him lose his composure and take a step back. Henry refocused and stepped forward spitting his tobacco onto Austin's shirt. Austin looked down at his shirt and then up to his left focusing across the street where he saw a group of men and women walking in separate directions. Some chuckled, some turned away, and none of them stopped.

"Abigail s'mine, boy." Henry stated as a fact before returning to the livery.

With as much dignity and self control as he could muster, Austin walked without a skip towards the town church.

Austin pushed open the heavy church door which never failed to cause a thunderous crash when it slammed closed. Fortunately, there were no services today which secretly made Austin happy. Why Father Eli allowed spittoons into the church he will never understand. Since it delighted the towns'people to 'miss', knowing that Austin would be on his hands and knees after every service scrubbing the floor clean.

Austin walked into the back of the empty church passing by the bedroom door of Old Father Eli who was busy trying to find the money to repair the aging pews.

"Good afternoon Austin." Father Eli said without having to look up.

"Good afternoon Father." Austin replied trying to cover the sound of anger and frustration in his voice, but the priest knew Austin too well. Father Eli stood from his budget and followed Austin to the young man's bedroom. From the doorway he saw Austin pulling his shirt off to take a better look at the tobacco stain left behind. He threw the shirt on his bed and grabbed the wash bucket that was typically used for the floors, poured water into it, grabbed his small washboard and setting to work the stain out before it completely set.

"Henry Lloyd?" Father Eli asked already knowing the answer.

"Henry Lloyd." Austin choked out the name.

Father Eli shook his head and for a moment cast his gaze down and smiled. Not a smile to mock Austin but one of recognition to the silly games that young men sometimes play on each other. Austin looked up to meet eyes with Father Eli whose kind old face and gentle manor always made Austin feel better.

"That young man has been your nemesis since you were six years old."

"As if Mama's passing wasn't enough for me at the time, he made damn sure that I knew my place."

"Don't swear."

"What am I going to do, upset the Lord? It seems like he's already unhappy with me."

Father Eli walked into the young man's room and sat down beside him as Austin continued to rigorously fight the stain.

"It's as if every time something happens that might make my life a little brighter, something always comes along to snatch away that fleeting moment of happiness. I don't understand, what could I have done that would have upset the Lord so that he would do this to me? I didn't ask to be what I am."

Father Eli thought for a moment. "Tell me what happened."

Austin took a deep breath and slowed his frustrated washing.

"I haven't spoken to you about this, but recently I've been trying to court a young lady."

"Young Miss Emerson?"

Austin looked up at Father Eli with surprise.

"I hear many things in confessionals. How long have you been interested in her?"

"Since the day she moved into town seven months ago. I thought that since she was new here that she could get to know me first as a person and not just know me as ... " Austin hated saying it. "... the bastard son of a whore."

Father Eli sympathized as he always did with Austin's status in the town. He felt the same old pinch in his heart because he could never tell Austin the truth. "Go on." Father Eli said.

"There's a dance tonight. I asked Abigail if she would let me escort her, and she said yes. I had never felt so happy in my life! I was on my way back here when... Henry Lloyd. He said that Abigail was his."

"What did Miss Emerson have to say about this?"

"She wasn't there. This was after I took my leave."

Father Eli smiled. "Laying claim on a young lady is not the same as laying claim on a parcel of land. Especially in regard to a young lady such as Miss Emerson. Whom, may I remind you, agreed to go with you to the dance, not Henry Lloyd.

Austin cracked a light smile. "True."

"Austin, I haven't spoken to you about this before but I suppose it's time. I have always believed that there was something special about you. When you were six and your mother passed, I took you in because I wanted to, not because it was my duty. The Lord has a plan for you. Something great, something... I can't even begin to imagine. You have grown up to be a good man and I am so proud of you. No matter what anyone else may say about you just because of who your mother was. That is not who you are. You're mother was a troubled girl, but she always loved you and did everything in her power to take care of you. I always felt the Lord took her home too soon, but you have to have faith in his will. The hardships you have suffered will bring you where you need to be when it's time. And, if that time is tonight to dance with a lovely young girl, then I say that a stain on your shirt is a small price to pay."

Father Eli placed his hand upon Austin, his son's, shoulder. "Now if you'll excuse me, I must somehow find the money to repair the pews in the back rows."

Father Eli stood and began to walk out of Austin's room.

"Thank you ,Father." Austin said with both meanings in mind.

"You're welcome, my son." Father Eli replied with both meanings in mind. "And, as far as Henry Lloyd is concerned, Young Miss Emerson would sooner accept the advances of a mule."

Austin smiled. Father Eli returned to his room to continue his budgeting. Austin looked down at his shirt and to his amazement the stain was gone.

Chapter 3

The Church Floor

The sound of hooves.
A stallion at full gallup through the night.
Another chasing minutes behind.

Despite jealous warnings from the yeti, Austin Baker successfully monopolized the dance card of the exquisite and angelically dressed Abigail Emerson for the evening. One perfect night filled with smiles and joy. Austin couldn't remember a time where he was ever so happy.

Lights.
Structures.
A town ahead.

The evening for Austin and Abigail drew to a close. The three and a half hours since they arrived had passed by so quickly. They left the barn where the dance was being held, hand in hand and casually strolled down the middle of the thoroughfare amidst light of the gas street lamps and the cold night air. The quiet was wonderful. Nearly the entire town was at the dance leaving the street scape all but empty for the couple to enjoy. Amidst the dim light of the gas lamps and the spectacular view of the star filled sky, Austin and Abigail finally had their first long awaited kiss.

Strange.
No one around.

Perhaps I can hide?
No one to see me.

The sound of heavy hooves drew Austin and Abigail's attention away from each other as a rider blew into town as fast as the horse he was on could carry. The couple stood so close as the rider passed they would have lost an arm had they extended one. They watched as the rider turned a corner just before the church and they could hear the horse come to a sudden halt.

"Perhaps it's a pony expressman arriving later than expected and trying to make up time." Abigail suggested.

It wasn't unheard of, but something just felt wrong. Not the appearance of a man racing towards something, but rather away. Austin started to take a step forward when they heard the sound of another horses 'gallup echoing from the pitch desert night. Austin and Abigail watched another rider appear from the blackness. This one seemed different. An air of authority and determination. Austin stepped out to the street in view of the new rider who stopped a short distance away. The glint of a badge reflected off the gas light.

"Have you seen a man ride through here?!" The rider asked with commanding intent.

Confounded, Austin answered honestly. "Yes sir, just a moment ago. He turned down that way." He said pointing to the street. "Then it sounded like he stopped -- What has happened?"

The rider produced a six shooter from inside his long duster and strained his eyes to focus in the low light. Never taking his gaze from the surroundings the rider slowly and quietly dismounted and guided his horse to the nearest hitching post where the exhausted mare was more than happy to take advantage of the water trough. Austin and Abigail backed away from the middle of the street clutching each other more tightly than before. Austin examined the man's badge more closely. It read U.S. Marshal embossed on the circular shield.

"Marshal, are you chasing a fugitive?" Austin asked almost innocently.

The Marshal didn't respond. Instead he moved within the shadows focusing on the street Austin had pointed to. He looked in all directions to try to catch the faint glint of iron aimed in his direction or perhaps the condensation from a man's breath coming from where it shouldn't.

A sudden bang, not the sound of gunfire but of a heavy wood door slamming shut. A sound that Austin was all too familiar with.

"Who would go into the church at this hour?" When Austin finished the question all the color drained out of the Marshal's face.

"Lord, please not again!" The Marshal could barely make the words. His body bolted towards the church as fast as he could before his mind could think.

"Abigail, stay here!" Austin barked to Abigail as he broke out of her grip and followed the Marshal. The endless seconds piled one on the other as the two men crossed the distance to the church door. Foolishly without caution and without thought of consequences the Marshal pushed through the inward opening door with Austin immediately behind. The heavy door slammed again making it's familiar sound. At the pulpit stood Father Eli beside... Him. The Marshal drew his pistol and aimed at the man who stood within inches of the priest who was just as stunned as Austin to the rapid turn of events.

That face.
I hate that face.

"Marshal Boone!" The Outlaw said with a smile that could make a man's blood run cold. Clean shaven apart from an Irish red goatee, long flowing reddish brown hair that any vain woman would sell their soul to possess, fair skinned, almost but not quite pale and strangely spared the brunt of the elements. Teeth white as snow and visible even in the candle lit church, all making his true age difficult to tell. An attractive man, one who clearly made his appearance a priority, and then the eyes. Almost charming in a way, reflecting a deep satisfaction to the moment at hand as if he was glad to see the Marshal who was chasing him and even pleased that a gun was pointed at his head.

"It is absolutely capital to see you again!" The Outlaw's smile continued.

Here, now, the Marshal is ready, but he still needs some encouragement.
I need to see it.

The Marshal slowly stepped forward.

"Priest, step away from him!" The Marshal barked.

"Oh, no..." The Outlaw gently put his right arm around Father Eli and gently laid his hand on the priest's far shoulder just below the man's neck. "The priest and I are old friends, aren't we Eli? That's why I came here. To see old friends"

Austin's gaze turned to Father Eli whose body tensed and shivered at the touch of this familiar hand upon his shoulder.

"That can't be! I've known Father Eli my whole life, and he's never mentioned anyone the likes of you before!" Austin's heart began to twist slightly.

"You're whole life?" The outlaw realized. "You must be -- Austin Baker! How you've grown." The chill started by the smile slipped deeper in and mocking tone became instantly insufferable. "Well, 'Father Eli 'has had other lives, boy."

"Get away from the priest!" The Marshal shouted enraged.

Austin could see the anguish on Father Eli's face as the Priest beheld the confusion and pain cast by the boy he called son.

"What are you going to do Marshal? You know I'm wanted alive. Can't collect the reward if my head is all over Jesus here." The outlaw thumbed back at the statue on the altar.

"I DON'T CARE!!"

"Oh, I see. This isn't about a reward. This is about revenge, or is it justice? I always had trouble with those two." Through the taunts the outlaw watched the Marshal's eyes carefully.

It's time. Smile.

"Is it justice when you are the one dealing it to the person who helped you? Your wife was such a burden to you, and your children. They were so young. You're little girl, your son. So young... so ... soft."

The outlaw got what he was waiting for. That brief look in a man's eyes in that moment just before they pull the trigger. That moment where there is no more doubt, no more confusion. The certainty that squeezing the trigger is absolutely the right choice. There are very few people in the world who have seen that look and even fewer who have lived past it or ever want to see it again. Then there are the very few who go looking for it.

The outlaw yanked the priest hard. The Marshal squeezed the trigger. The gun fired. Father Eli was in the way.

In one fluid motion the outlaw drew the revolver on his left side, pulled the hammer back with his thumb and set loose a ball of lead into the eye of the Marshal. The outlaw released Father Eli and the two men on opposite ends of the church fell to the floor. The moment had left Austin petrified, when it passed he cried out with a wail to make angels weep. The outlaw stood aside, still holding the pistol in his left hand as he examined Austin and felt the crashing waves of loss wash over him. The soft silk of Austin's screeching howls calmed the outlaw's heart as a tear fell from his eye in the appreciation of such exquisite beauty.

Austin charged to Father Eli whose soul had not yet left the earth as evident from his gasps and wheezing of air coming from the hole in his chest. Austin fell beside him and turned Father Eli up causing him to cough blood into Austin's face. The outlaw watched as the joyous satisfaction built inside of him, taking deep breaths and closing his eyes so he could immerse himself in the music. The outlaw took one last deep breath in through his nose and out through his mouth before he opened his eyes and turned to leave.

"Forgive me son." Said Father Eli with all of his strength.

"You're forgiven, Father." The outlaw replied while sauntering away in his grading apathy and mocking tone as he began humming to himself.

"I will send you to Hell you son of a bitch! I promise I will find you and make you burn forever!" Austin shouted.

The outlaw stopped just before the door and turned back.

That smile again. "I like you. Already it begins again. Thank you."

He returned his attention to the door, pulled hard against it's weight which crashed behind him with that familiar wooden thud.

Austin's attention returned to the priest. Father Eli slowly blinked once, coughed, blinked once more and then stopped coughing.

Austin wept.

Then the sound of a woman screaming outside the church. Austin's fear returned as he laid his Father's head down and raced to the door. The sound of galloping hooves heading off into the night with the screams accompanying their hasty departure. He could see the faint silhouette of a horse and rider with a touch of something white. Austin frantically looked around yelling "Abigail!" with no reply. Austin charged back into the church and took the Marshal's gun which was still clutched by dead hands. Austin ran back out towards the Marshal's horse. He unwrapped the reigns from the hitching post, mounted the mare and commanded her to go. However, she was a smart mare, and would only let one particular U.S. Marshal ride her. She bucked and stood up throwing the unsuspecting Austin from her back onto the hard ground. He felt the ground come up to meet him, then all quickly faded black.

Chapter 4

Mister Emmerson

Austin's eyes snapped open. He looked around to see the familiar setting of his small uncluttered room in the back of the church. It was early morning by the direction of the fingers of light peering through his single small window. In that moment he thanked the Lord that it was all just a terrible dream, and then he tried to sit up. His head was thick and pain shot from his back in every direction. He cried out as he fell back onto the bed gaining the attention of Doc Lambert who had been outside in the hall. Once, another lifetime ago, Julian Lambert was a field medic in the war for southern independence. Except, Doc Lambert was on the side that 'won'. He tried to get away from that life after the war ended, but fate had other plans for him as his skills continued to draw him to those in need. Despite the fact that Julian Lambert had seen more blood, severed limbs, and heard enough cries of pain and terror to make a man awaken with nightmares every morning of his life, he returned to the profession of surgeon. When he started helping people again, the terrible dreams went away.

"Austin?" Doc Lambert said as he sat gently beside the him. "How are you feeling, son?"

"I - My back --", and then he remembered. "Father Eli... Where's Abigail?!"

"You tell us. She was last seen with you leaving the dance last night." Said from the man who just entered the room behind Doctor Lambert. Solid gold pocket watch and fob tucked into the finest waist coat, and cloaked in a well tailored frock and a high collared shirt supporting the head with his ever present bushy sideburns, tightly curled and greying hair, and face trained to command the obedience of the hundreds under his employ. The father of miss Abigail, Mister Preston Emerson.

"She was -- He took her!" Austin fought through the pain from his back which he was starting to get used to.

"Who?!" Mister Emerson questioned with a calm but determined authority. Through his stiffness, back pain, and tears of loss, Austin recounted the events of the previous night about the outlaw, the marshal, the death of Father Eli and how the outlaw must have taken Abigail after Austin told her to remain outside. Mister Emerson listened carefully to Austin's story making sure to note every detail no matter how slight. When the story was finished Mister Emerson said nothing, simply turned and walked out of Austin's room. Austin could hear a large group of men outside his door standing in the main part of the church where Austin last saw Father Eli. Mister Emerson barked orders to the men describing the outlaw as Austin had recounted the description of him and his horse. Austin heard the large group of men leave by the front door of the church which slammed as it always did when the last had gone.

"Father Eli... The Marshal..." Austin asked Doc Lambert.

"I'm sorry son." Doc Lambert said with all sincerity as he had so many times before.

"I know." Austin replied. "I took the Marshal's gun..."

"Son, you are in no condition to go searching for Miss Emerson."

"Would that stop you?"

"I suppose not." Doc Lambert helped Austin to his feet. "When you fell from the horse you got the wind knocked out of you, maybe some cracked ribs and a slight bump on the head. If you rest you should be all right."

"I can't rest, Julian." Austin saw that the gun he had taken from the marshal was sitting on his dresser, the marshal's blood still spattered on it. He picked it up with no thought of the blood and slowly walked out of his room using the wall to balance his steps. Reaching the now empty main hall he saw that the marshal and Father Eli had already been taken away. The blood still staining the floor.

"They were taken to my place." Doc Lambert said. "Old James is digging the ..." He stopped himself and took a breath. "... The funeral is later today."

Austin stared at the pulpit where he held Father Eli in his arms as he died. He couldn't pull his eyes away as the tears started to flow again.

"Austin, maybe you should..."

"No!" Austin focused and wiped his face with his sleeve, and then continued stronger out the front door, aching under the weight as he pulled it open.

The sun couldn't have been up for more than a couple of hours. Mister Emerson stood facing towards the horizon as he watched the hired men on horseback heading out to find Abigail. Already half the town was gathered outside the church, many of them weeping as the men brought their hats to their chests and the women cried into hankies of various quality depending on their status in the town. Some disliked Austin for what he was, but no one really hated him, except for maybe Henry Lloyd who was strangely absent from the group of towns people outside the church. Nor was he with the search party that had just left. The town knew that Eli was the father Austin never had. Austin had always been a man of integrity, even when the towns people weren't especially polite to him. However, it was not Austin, but Father Eli whom they came to mourn and pray for.

Austin lumbered towards Mister Emerson as able as he could with Doc Lambert close behind.

"Mister Emerson?" Austin said as respectfully as he could with a splitting headache and bruised ribs.

"Yes, Mister Baker." No one had ever called Austin, Mister Baker before.

"You own the livery as well as many other businesses in town. I would like to ask for a horse so I can help find your daughter." Austin asked through his pained breathing.

Mister Emerson had no distain for Austin as the other members of the town did, but he had no intention of letting the man who endangered his daughter to go out and find her, no matter how noble the sentiment. However, rather than let Austin's passion go to waste, he decided to use him like any good businessman would.

"Mister Baker, the twenty trackers, bounty hunters and law men I could find at such short notice are all far more skilled at locating outlaws than you are. Secondly, you can barely stand, which denotes your current ability to ride a horse. Your gesture of assistance is appreciated. However, I believe more can be accomplished by finding information about this outlaw who abducted my daughter. That is how you can help." Mister Emerson took his leave without further word and escorted by aides returned in the direction of his home.

Doc Lambert stepped forward beside Austin and tried to read his profile. The look of a young man faced with horrors that he was unaccustomed to dealing with. Doc Lambert had seen it all too often as his thoughts drifted back to his time in the war.

"I want to see Eli." Austin nearly whispered.

Concealed from the second story window of a nearby hotel, a familiar and detested set of eyes cooly watched Austin and the town Doctor walk slowly away from the church. So sadistically curious to see the effects of his actions, the man returned to the town he had just left after having relieved himself of the young blonde burden. He drew a patch of long, freshly cut hair from his pocket and held it to his nose, breathing deeply. Then he returned to the writing desk, dipped the quill into an ink bottle, and re- sumed composing his ever expanding symphony.

Chapter 5

Wanted

Doc Lambert's place was just a little house with two rooms. A small one cot bedroom and the larger room which in any other house one would normally find soft chairs and entertain guests. Not here. Three long tables dominated the room with a china cabinet serving as Doc Lambert's equipment case. The tools of medicine had changed little since the war and many of his surgical instruments had seen action in the battlefield. The old blood stains on the wooden floor beneath the tables could never be scrubbed clean despite Doc Lambert's repeated attempts. There was also a strange sort of smell of something that wasn't quite rotting mixed with laudanum. Two of the tables were occupied. The late Marshal Boone on the right table by the wall with a cloth over his face, and the beloved Father Eli laid peacefully on the center table.

Austin stood beside Father Eli without crying. Doc Lambert watched Austin's face turn red as a savage while his eyes fixed on Eli's now pale face. He didn't move for nearly an hour. Just stayed motionless ignoring everything that was around him and anything that Doc Lambert had said. Lambert left Austin alone and went to work on the Marshal cleaning the head wound and trying to make him look as presentable as he could with the man's missing eye. Doc Lambert noted in his journal that he could see the table through the Marshal's head.

As Doc Lambert continued to prepare the Marshal for burial, he noticed something inside the breast pocket of the Marshal's duster. Upon reveal the item was a stack of papers containing a small journal and a distressed wanted poster that looked like it had been folded and unfolded a thousand times.

WANTED ALIVE TO STAND TRIAL
RICHARD KETCHUM
a.k.a. "Slippery Rick"
For
ROBBERY, MURDER, KIDNAPPING, ASSAULT
ON WOMEN AND CHILDREN AND
ACTS OF INDIGNITY
$2000
REWARD

Above the list of crimes was a somewhat decently drawn face of a man with long hair, a goatee and unpleasant eyes.

"Austin." Doc Lambert said as he brought the poster to Austin's attention. It took a moment for him to lift his head, but when he did Austin's eye color had turned from blue to grey when he saw the poster. Snatching it from Doc Lambert's hand Austin examined every line of the sketch. His face turned even redder than it was before. Beads of sweat formed on his head as he gripped the fragile yellowing paper tightly with his calloused hands.

That face. I hate that face.

"I also found this." Doc Lambert handed Austin the small journal. It didn't take long to realize that this was the chronicle of Marshal Boone's pursuit of Richard Ketchum and the reasons for the Marshal's intense hatred of the outlaw. Austin stopped himself from reading it and pushed the small journal into his pocket. Then he took another painful glare at the wanted poster before folding it with it's well worn lines back into a smaller rectangle and pushed it into the same pocket with the journal.

"When will he be ready for the services?" Austin asked absently as his mind raced with dark thoughts pushing the pain down.

"They'll be ready by three o'clock." Doc Lambert replied.

Without another word, Austin took the Marshal's gun belt and left the makeshift hospital.

∞

Nearly the entire town was in attendance. The church was so full there was only enough seats for half of the people. Father Eli was placed for the viewing almost at the same location he was killed. Beside him the open casket of Marshal Boone with a cloth partially covering his face where the bullet wound was. Normally, Father Eli was the one leading people in prayer and mourning when a loved one passed away. Now there was a sense of being lost with no one to lead the towns people. Austin could barely stand to be in the church as he sat in the back row. A torrent of fury ripped through him as the towns people whose lives were uplifted by the work Father Eli had done spoke to his memory. He thought he knew the man better than anyone but now he couldn't even find the words to honor his life. This outlaw hinted Father Eli as possibly being something more sinister. The betrayal Austin felt was nearly as strong as the anger he was using to bury the pain. Along with the overwhelming sorrow, his deep concern he felt for Abigail and being forbidden by her father to help look for her made him even more frustrated and confused. He didn't realize at first when they called him to the front of the church to speak. After the third time they called his name he finally looked up. There was just too much to say.

∞

What is taking them all so long?
The observer from the second story window thought to himself. The doors of the church finally opened. First emerged the casket of what looked like Father Eli. It seemed a likely guess since

Austin was the front pallbearer. Watching as they lumbered out with the first and finally the second casket. The observer drew his hat from his head and closed his eyes for a moment to honor the passing of such exciting people, and excited yet again to have someone new in his life. If he follows suit, that is. Also, if the timing is right, the last nail in the coffin should be arriving any time now.

So excited.

Chapter 6

Her Bedroom Door

"It's so cool today...."
Take a step forward.
"The sky is so clear and still..."
Take a step forward.
"I wonder what Daddy had for breakfast..."
Take a step forward.
"I'd love some eggs..."
Take a step forward.
"I wonder what all those people are doing..."
Take a step forward.

A woman gasped. Not sure which one, but it brought the others attention to what she saw. A young lady in what was once a beautiful white dress slowly approached the crowd. Her swollen face, cracked dry lips, a bit of hair missing, and focusing every bit of concentration she had to put one foot in front of the other as she seemed to just appear in the center of the thoroughfare. Through the crowd a young man shoved and pushed, screaming for everyone to get out of his way. Austin emerged from the crowd ignoring his back and ribs aching for him to stop.

"Abigail!" He cried out.

Austin reached her and in his haste all but ignored the way she appeared. He threw his arms around the girl in a moment of joyous relief. Abigail failed to respond. Her face was so bruised. Half of her hair was missing, and by he look of it, cut off by a knife. Her dress was covered in dry mud and dirt, torn from the waist all the way down the front and stained with the color of blood. Austin held her tight for the last time. A moment of panic shot from her swollen eyes and raspy voice when she screamed. Such a scream. Her arms flailed about shoving and throwing Austin away who let go out of confusion and fear. She turned around and around staring at everything failing to recognize where she was. She saw all the familiar towns people who had just left the burial of the Marshal and Father Eli, and didn't know a single one of them. Even the distraught young man who stood with his arms outstretched and pained. Her heart and instinct told her that she could only do one thing, she ran.

Austin, Doc Lambert, and several other towns people followed Abigail in her plight as she half ran, half stumbled and screaming all the way. Somehow she reached her house. Through the tears, the swollen eyes and the hysteria she recognized Home and threw open the front door, bolted down the hall into her bedroom and slammed the door shut. Quickly following was the sound of a heavy piece of furniture scraping along the floor and a shadow covering the bottom space of the door.

"What on Earth is this?!" Mister Emerson shouted as Austin burst through the open doorway and down the hall to the door he glimpsed Abigail shut behind her. Mister Emerson only heard the door flung open and hadn't seen his daughter enter.

"Mister Baker, this is outrag--!"

"Abigail!" Austin banged on the door. "ABIGAIL!!"

"She's here?!" Mister Emerson said with wide eyes and hope.

"She's been hurt. She screamed and ran here." Doc Lambert told the young lady's father.

They could hear the sound of Abigail wailing beyond the door.

"Abigail?! Abby Joe! This is your Father! Let me in! Please Abby!"

"Get away from me! Don't touch me!! Don't Touch Me!! Poppa! POPPA!! NO!" She screamed.

Austin and Mister Emerson along with other men in the town who followed pushed against the door together against the armoire Abigail had shoved in front of it. It took all of their strength to push against the sold oak mass. It later baffled them how the slight build of a young lady was able to slide it over in the first place. When they finally got in, Abigail was curled up in the corner furthest from the door tightly clutching the brass bed-warmer in hand and continuing to wail and scream for someone to stop who wasn't there. Mister Emerson and Austin approached slowly as the other men watched from the doorway.

"Abby, it's me. It's Poppa." Mister Emerson's voice had been so accustomed to barking orders that even his gentlest tone sounded like a command. Abigail slowed her wailing and slowly opened her swollen and bruised eyes as best she could. Even in her blurred hysteria she was able to recognize her father's voice and face. One hand continued its 'firm grip on the bed warmer while the other reached out. Poppa took Abby Joe's hand and came in close to protect his little girl from the terrible monsters again.

"Mis'er Emerson?" A woman's voice called from behind the gawking pack of men and the desperately concerned Austin.

"Gloria." Mister Emerson responded to the negro servant woman without looking up. "Please escort these gentlemen out of our home." Not a gentle request. A regular command.

"Yes sir, Mis'er Emerson." Miss Gloria followed her instructions and shooed the others out. Austin remained assuming he was not included in the order to leave.

"Abigail. It's Austin."

"Thank you for your assistance Mister Baker. I will take care of my daughter now." Another command.

"But --"

"Come on son..." Miss Gloria placed her hands on Austin's shoulders and gave a gentle pull. "Miss Abigail needs some rest now."

Mister Emerson's attention turned back to his daughter. In his mind, Austin had already gone even though he was still beside them. Reluctantly he gave way to the gentle persuasion of Miss Gloria's touch and stood up. His heart and mind returned to the state of confusion and anger it had been in all day. Miss Gloria took Austin out the front door and down the cobblestone path leading to the street.

"I promise if she asks for you, I will find you fast as lightning." Miss Gloria said, even though Austin didn't ask.

"Thank you." Took so much effort for him to say.

Miss Gloria walked back in the house and respectfully closed the front door. Austin thought to return to the church to tell Father Eli what had happened, then he remembered. There was still something of a crowd outside the Emerson home and they all watched as Austin broke down, fell to his knees and wept still more tears.

Night had come and the sun rose again, but Austin hadn't slept. He sat on the dirt at the end of the cobblestone path leading to the front door of the Emerson home. Some of the town's people brought him blankets and food through the night but Austin refused to eat anything. The morning activity of the town began as people were stepping outside their front doors, emptying their commodes onto the street and stretching their legs to take in the morning air and begin the day's work. The normal things that people do every day as if yesterday never happened. Wagons entered town from the West. Fir traders, cowboys, a group of musicians, a peddler selling his miracle potions. Then without realizing it, his eyes closed and he dreamed.

∞

"Follow him." Said Father Eli.

Austin's eyes snapped open with the day half gone. Someone had the kindness and foresight to cover Austin's head and face with a blanket to shield him from the sun along with a bucket of water and a cup while he was sleeping. Flowers and gifts were left at the end of the cobblestone path. He realized that someone was standing beside him and the gifts. A towering menace of hair and the less than delightful smell of sweat and horse manure could only come from one person. Austin didn't bother to stand up. There was nothing the bully could do to intimidate him anymore.

Henry Lloyd looked down at Austin. Looked, not glared for the first time that Austin could remember. He also went without a single condescending or idiotic word coming out of his mouth, another surprise. Henry Lloyd just stood there trying to form words. His tobacco stained teeth would be exposed for a moment as the beginning of a sound would be uttered, and then slip back under the over growth. After an annoying period of time Henry finally gave the impression that he might be human after all.

"It ain't right." said Henry, and returned to his previous mode of silence.

When several more moments of uncomfortable silence passed, Henry thought that he wouldn't get a response so he began to turn and walk away.

"Henry." Austin said.

Henry stopped.

"What would you do?"

Henry though about it his answer, yet another new development.

"Austin... I'm a coward." Henry could feel the words burning the back of his throat as they came out. They were especially painful because they were true.

"You're brave. Braver than I am, and that's why I've hated you all these years. My pa fought in da war. He died a war hero and I couldn't live up to that. But, you didn't need a war. You did da right thing savin 'those women and children n 'all I could do was hide behind a rock and watch..." Henry took a deep breath. "...Just like I watched him take Miss Abigail."

Austin's attention focused coldly on Henry's unappealing face. Henry took another deep breath.

"I followed the two of you from da dance. I saw da both've the men on the horses and I saw you go in da church. I heard da guns and I saw Abigail. She stayed right where you told her to and dinn't move. When da man ran out and got his horse, I thought he'd done shot all you. I reckon Miss Abigail thought that too. She started towards the church. That man came around with da horse and picked her up. He was so fast and I was... I was so scared I couldn't move. Then I saw you run out 'the church and get on that Marshal's horse. I saw that mare buck you off. You weren't movin. I thought you were dead, and I... I ran away. I ran home and I been there since, too scared to come out."

Austin's expression didn't change through Henry's confession. He never turned red and scarcely a noticeable breath. A shorter moment of silence passed.

"What would you do?" Austin repeated the question with the exact intonations as the first time.

"Me... I'd run 'way. You... You'd get justice for Miss Abigail n' Father Eli."

Austin went flush. The paleness his skin had developed from the past two days seemed to vanish in seconds, his normal color returned and he took air deep into his lungs as if it was for the first time.

"Thank you, Henry." Were the last words Austin expected to ever say and Henry Lloyd ever expected to hear. Henry blinked in amazement without words to say. He returned to his departure and walked off in the direction of the livery.

Austin stood up for the first time since falling to his knees in tears the day before. He ignored the stiffness and pins as blood returned to his legs as he walked down the cobblestone path to the Emerson front door. The knock was full of purpose and determination. Miss Gloria opened the door with strict instructions that no one be let in.

"I'm sorry Mis'er Austin, Miss Abigail still isn't receiving."

"I'm not here to see Abigail. I want to speak to Mister Emerson." With such cool purpose his voice commanded obedience almost the same way as Mister Emerson's. Miss Gloria asked Austin to wait on the porch rather then allow him into the foyer. He watched as Miss Gloria went down the hall to Abigail's room and knocked gently on the door.

"Mis'er Emerson. Mis'er Baker here to see you sir." She announced through the closed door.

A few muffled words from both Mister Emerson and Abigail could be heard but not interpreted from behind the door and down the main hall. The door opened in angry haste.

"I told you, she is not receiving visitors!"

"Mis'er Baker is want'n to see you, sir."

Mister Emerson's head poked out from the bedroom door, followed by his body as he swiftly closed Abigail's door behind him.

"No one goes in there." He barked.

"Yes, sir." Miss Gloria stood vigil outside Abigail's room.

Inconvenienced and offended, Preston Emerson stomped down the hallway to the open front door where Austin remained patiently waiting.

"Yes, Mister Baker?" Mister Emerson said with every expectation that Austin would expediently declare the purpose of this crude interruption.

"Mister Emerson, I understand that amongst many other things, you own the livery in town."

"Yes." Mister Emerson replied with a little more intrigue in his voice.

"I would like to request a horse, saddle and supplies to be billed to me at a later date."

"To what purpose?"

"Justice for Father Eli, and your daughter."

Chapter 7

Last Look

It had been four days since the murder of Father Eli and the brutal violation of Miss Abigail. Around him was a sight Austin had never expected in his lifetime. The whole town had come out to see him off. Many spared a little and brought him food, water, money, clothes, and supplies for his journey. He had publicly vowed to bring the outlaw to justice. Duplicates were made of the wanted poster by the local newspaper and placed all over town with a much more accurate rendering of Richard Ketchum's face. The man who did this needed to be caught. He needed to be punished.

Mister Emerson had come to the decision to help after Austin had showed him the wanted poster found with the Marshal. Assuming he didn't return, Mister Emerson was only out a sixty dollar horse but also a brave young man whose courting of his daughter always secretly infuriated him until now. He had misjudged Austin. Like many others he believed the boy was nothing more than the tainted son of a call girl who was taken in by the town priest because no one else would be saddled with the shame of his origins. He believed his daughter's fancy of Austin was nothing more than her attempt to rebel against his wishes, like daughters sometimes do. He began to understand what Abigail had seen in the young man. Austin was not what the unflattering stories would lead you to believe. It all came down to a matter of honor. If Austin succeeded, then there would be one less lunatic in the world

bringing misery into other people's lives. More over, Father Eli
would be avenged and his daughter's honor would be restored.

Austin secured the saddle and the other supplies. He chose carefully as not to overload his horse and made sure to bring only
what he absolutely needed. Years ago, Austin took a job moving
herds of cattle from Albuquerque to Santa Fe for three seasons.
Not a long trip by the standards of other cattle drives, but Austin
learned how to live off the land and take care of himself.

It wasn't easy for the town's people to see him go. Many of them
had had been so unfair to Austin over the years. Yet, that's simply
how it was. So many of them could not forgive him for something
that was never his doing. We never choose where we come from,
we never choose our parents, we never choose where and how we
enter this world. Life is thrust upon us and tests our caliber to
either rise above the challenges or be crushed beneath their heels.
Yet we still find time to judge our neighbors for their own origins
regardless if they have done everything in their power to embrace or escape them. We sit complacent in our lives, unwilling
to change and always willing to cast stones at those who are con-
sidered less than we are. All of that changed in just a few days.

The bastard son of a whore was no longer the black sheep of the
town. He was a man. A braver man than most had given him
credit for and braver than any could know, and this might be the
last time any of them would see him. He had made his choice. He
would pursue this demon in human form and challenge him with
nothing but his wits. He also vowed not to make the same mistake Marshal Boone did. There was a strong sense of madness to
the whole endeavor. Austin knew that. The man he was chasing
was a murderer and worse, but Austin understood why the Marshal was pursuing this outlaw. He wasn't just a criminal or a man
whose hard life made him callous. He was an evil set loose upon
the world that will continue to bring pain, chaos and death to all
those who crossed his path. Austin's mission was clear. Destroy
the evil or die trying.

Austin mounted his new horse who went by the name of Jackson, the finest stud in the livery. Mister Emerson made sure that Austin got the best he could. Surrounded by the towns people who came to see him off, Austin's final connection to his home was in the teary eyes of a nine year old girl named Elizabeth holding her mother's hand. Always a dear and always with a smile on her face, until today. He didn't know whether she truly understood the depth of what Austin was doing, but she cried nonetheless.

A gentle tap on the side from Austin's boot and Jackson began to walk. As they headed to the edge of town Austin and Jackson passed the Emerson home. At the start of the cobblestone path stood Mister Emerson watching with new found respect for the young man. He set aside his prideful arrogance and stepped out to meet Austin. Jackson halted without command as if already knowing. The expressions on the two men's faces didn't require words. Simply extended hands which were shaken for the first, and perhaps last time. Austin glanced over to the window of the house, somehow hoping that Abigail would be there to at least see him off or perhaps even run out to him to stop him.

Nothing.
She wasn't there.

Jackson again felt the familiar tap on his side and began to trot. The journal of Marshal Boone said that Richard Ketchum was partial to California and the new Arizona Territory. So the direction to start was west.

Don't look back.
There is only forward now.

The day had ended and the town had long since gone to sleep for the night. Over an hour had passed since the gas lamps had been doused leaving only the half moonlight to see. In the near darkness, a long haired man lead his horse quietly down the thoroughfare humming softly, then he would make a mistake, angrily stop, start over and correct the tune until it was perfect. Sketches of his likeness on wanted posters donned every building he passed. Even in through the dim evening light he could see that the bounty had been raised to three-thousand dollars. The man felt insulted by the pithy amount.

As he neared the end of the thoroughfare he passed the finest home in town. The man stopped at the end of the cobblestone path which leading to the front porch. He appreciated the fine craftsmanship for some time as he let go of the horse's reigns and casually walked up the path to the front door, still humming his self composed tune. His head cocked to one side and then up again before he pulled a thick bundle of long blonde hair from his pocket. He held it to his nose and took one last deep breath be-fore laying the hair at the door's threshold. The man turned and resumed his humming as he walked down the path back to his horse. He mounted his steed and headed west out of town. He had to make sure his pursuer didn't get too far ahead of him.

Chapter 8

Arizona Territory, April 1880

"He will show you the way." Said Father Eli.

Austin's eyes snapped open. The morning sun having not yet peeked over the horizon and Austin had awoken from yet another dream. Always ends the same. Father Eli appearing in his bloodied clothes standing before Austin, beckoning. He rubbed his encrusted eyes hoping that the image of Father Eli would fade along with the rest of his increasingly vivid and strange dreams. Dreams of a strange town he had never seen in person or even in pictures. Images of faces he could not place and sights that faded from memory as quickly as the sleep left him.

The fire had gone out sometime during the night. The layers of wool blankets he had brought accompanied by three weeks without shaving had provided him with as much warmth was possible. Loyal and understanding Jackson slept nearby keeping him company. The relaxing sound of water trickling in a small brook Austin had found the day before. He stopped for a full day to rest, washed his cooking pan, his clothes and himself which all began to smell worse than Henry Lloyd did on a good day.

Crouching naked beside the water with a bar of soap in one hand vigorously rubbing a troubling stain on his pants, the brook became still for just a moment. Ripples faded into a nearly smooth sheet of glass. Austin's fright came from the stranger glaring back at him from beneath the waters 'surface. Long slicked wet hair, an unkempt overgrown beard obscuring all but the eyes watching him with such anger burning behind heavy storm clouds blocking the brilliance of the midday sun.

This man in the water's reflection was born three weeks ago when Austin Baker died. He inherited all of Austin's memories keeping them carefully locked away. Only pulling out the ones he needed as a frugal man draws money from a closely guarded coin purse. He even looked a bit like Austin Baker behind his scraggly face and a travel weathered body. The man had barely eaten since he was born. Once strong and healthy now clearly able to count the ribs beneath his skin. Upon seeing this stranger for the briefest moment he thought, I pity this man. What happened to him? How did he become this?

The flow of water returned and Austin cried for the first time since he left home.

∞

Following the clues within the pages of Marshal Boone's journal as to Richard Ketchum's path, Austin had crossed the invisible border into the new Arizona territory along the Beale Road. He was heading to a recently founded logger town called Flagstaff mentioned in the most recent entries as the last place the outlaw had been seen. Austin had never been out of the New Mexico territory and the only other town he had been to was Santa Fe. Now he could see this small town in the distance. Perhaps a days ride along the beaten path.

The scenery had changed so much from home. Surrounded by rocky hills, deer and the occasional bear, but it was the smell of an endless forest of pine Austin found overwhelming. His journey had been filled with long empty roads with no company but Jackson and the Marshal's journal. It was within the early pages that he learned what had happened to the poor man's family...

Many of the journal entries appeared as more letters to God and then later to the Marshal's wife Emma, as if she was still alive and well and simply far away. Through the entries, Austin learned how Marshal Boone followed the trail of Richard Ketchum for nearly two years from California to New Mexico. It became more clear that this was all some kind of game to the outlaw. Marshal Boone had crossed paths with other lives that had been torn apart by Ketchum through deceit, theft, rape and murder. The Marshal's frustration grew within the pages as he always seemed to be one step behind the outlaw, yet he kept good notes on where he'd been, what he'd done and how he believed the outlaw thought.

According to the journal Richard Ketchum appeared to be well educated. Fluent in Latin, Spanish, French, and even Mandarin along with English. On more than one occasion the Marshal also made note of the incessant humming. A tune apparently composed by the outlaw who even claimed once that he could never seem to get it quite right. Austin strained his memory trying to recall the melody that he barely heard as the outlaw was departing the church. It wasn't quite like any tune he had ever heard.

∞

The following day Austin arrived in the small booming town named Flagstaff. There was little to it, some few wood structures, what might be called a main thoroughfare, telegraph wires, plans for a new railroad line under construction, and a nearly completed post office all surrounded by forested hills and cattle ranches.

It wasn't like home. Settlers moving their worldly belongings in covered wagons was something he saw from time to time but not like here. A makeshift emporium was most popular as it was the one structure besides the brothel that there was a line out the door. Austin dismounted and took Jackson by the reigns and the two of them took in the sights.

"So Jackson, Ever seen the like?"

Jackson huffed in response.

"Me neither."

Strolling through the muddy thoroughfare was one of the few familiar things Austin took notice of, and how Abigail always tried so hard to avoid the mud. How beautiful she was even hoisting her dress in an undignified fashion to keep the spattering off her white...

Austin shook his head and took a deep breath to focus. He began by asking someone in line at the emporium if there was a sheriff or a marshal in the town.

"Sometimes." A rude portly man snipped, hair black as coal, dirty arms folded and taking no more than a passing glance at the inquirer.

The 1st of February, 1880

Dearest Emma,

I arrived in a rancher town this afternoon having lost Ketchum's trail three days ago upon leaving a mining camp to the South, I forget the name. There was something queer about the place. Friendly people but not quite right in the head. I did behold an ingenious idea at the local watering hole. Tom, the proprietor of the saloon took a windmill connected to some crazy mechanical contrivance which caused fans blow the air inside the saloon to keep it cool on hot days. Tom even claimed that the contrivance associated with an iron box behind the bar kept his liquor cool without ice. I don't know how it worked but it was nice to get a cold shot of whiskey. I know you don't like me drinking. Please forgive my trespass. You would have enjoyed the marvelous invention. I left the small mining camp after Tom spoke of a man arriving the day before who by description could be Richard Ketchum. He stated that Ketchum said he was heading north to Flagstaff after a conversation with Tom about why the camp had no church. Tom had also mentioned his disquiet and that he wanted nothing more than to move the stranger along out of his establishment.

The name of the logger town is Flagstaff. I'm bedding down for the night after a stop at the bath house to wash. I plan to call on the local law tomorrow and find out if he may have been here. I just can't keep the sandman away any more. Kiss the children for me. I miss you all and I'll be home soon.

With all my love,

Bill

The 4th of February 1880

The local sheriff was little more than a brigand without character or influence capable of hypocritically sorting only minor scuffles between the drunken buffoons frequenting the local Saloon. A piece of luck fell before me when a woman seeking some assistance in locating her missing husband overheard my description of Ketchum to the sheriff. She described a small group of exceptionally talented band of musicians who had left town not a week prior with one member matching the description. She claimed that they had been in town for months performing at the saloon until their long haired dandy of a composer returned. It was also the day the woman's husband went missing. She said he would spend nearly every evening at the saloon hearing the musicians perform. I believed the disappearance of the woman's husband was important. I know that Ketchum can wear many faces so I sat with her and asked everything I could about him and the long haired dandy.

The woman, Margaret, and her husband Ronald Svenson had been married eight years. Her suspicions of his infidelity were born from his interest in the vocal talents of one young lady who was the main performer of the group. Margaret and her husband had argued the evening he failed to return home. She claims that he struck her before he left which would account for the healing bruise below her left eye. After Ronald's departure, Margaret went looking for him in the town where she noticed the long haired dandy gathering his troupe for a hasty departure. She also overheard the long haired dandy say Albuquerque before they boarded the wagon and set out into the night. This was also the last night Margaret had seen her husband...

"Does anyone know a woman named Margaret Svenson?" Austin asked to anyone who would listen. Half a dozen people in line turned to Austin including the portly man all suddenly more interested than they were a moment ago.

"What you want with 'er?" The portly man asked.

"I'm looking for someone. I hear tell she might know how to find him."

"The long haired dandy and his musical entourage?" Another man in line said as if annoyed that he even had to ask.

"Yes, How did you know that?" Austin replied after a moments surprise.

The portly man let out a deep sigh and rolled his eyes, "That woman has dun 'nuthin 'but go on and on about 'That Long Haired Dandy ..." The portly man relocked eyes with Austin. "You a bounty hunter?"

Austin paused, "Yes." He lied.

"Come'n by which way?"

"Albuquerque."

"I reckon that Marshal never caught 'em then."

"Marshal Boone is dead. He was murdered by the long haired dandy." Austin's deadpan statement caught more attention from the other people in line. Even the rude portly man changed his tone when he heard.

"He also murdered a priest..." Austin took a deep breath and squeezed Jackson's reigns tight enough to hurt. "...and then raped and beat a young lady. Now, she screams if anyone tries to touch her." The horse with his amazing intuition nudged his snout on Austin's shoulder.

"Lord in heaven... Who is this awful man?" A woman in line stated.

"He's not a man, he is the devil. I'd be grateful if anyone knows anything about the long haired dandy to come find me." Austin said as he gently tugged on Jackson's reigns to continue the stroll along the thoroughfare.

"You'll find the widow Svenson work'n to ready the new post office, If'n she's not spend'n time with the Sheriff try'n to get him to look for her dead husband's killer." The portly bitter man said aloud.

"Thank you sir." Austin replied.

∞

She was attractive, was being the appropriate word. The widow Svenson had since healed from the injuries reported of in the Marshal's journal, but that didn't take into account the appearance that she had been dragged by a wild horse across jagged rocks. Austin's thoughts drew back to some of the whores who worked back in Albuquerque. They had been beaten and sometimes maimed by their patrons and the damage was almost always visible long afterwards. He also remembered to how they always enjoyed his company since he was the only man who didn't partake in their services. He couldn't and wouldn't because of his mother, and the whores loved him for it. It was clear the widow Svenson had felt the force of her husband's anger on many occasions.

"Ma'am?" Austin tipped his hat.

"Yes sir, can I help you?" The widow responded, halting her task of organizing a stack of letters.

"My name is Austin Baker Ma'am. If I may ask, are you the widow Svenson?"

"Yes." Without the slightest hesitation.

"I'd like to ask you about your husband."

"Did you find him?" With a touch more concern than enthusiasm.

"Not yet. I would like to know more about the night your husband disappeared."

"I see, Are you working with Marshal Boone?"

"I've – – taken over the search for your husband's murderer."

"I see." Her face became porcelain. Austin noticed.

"You said the man who murdered your husband was a long haired dandy." It wasn't a question.

"Yes. That's right."

"What was his manner?"

"Well, he was a tall man. Long straight brown hair with a short red beard. I'd seen him before, you see, with those other musicians playing over at that wretched saloon. He would come and go but the others would stay there, singing and playing that ungodly music. A gentleman for the most part. Always so respectful to everyone and the finest smile this side of San Francisco."

"Ungodly music?"

"It wasn't good Christian music, I tell you! All those abhorrent saloon girls at the Donahue presenting their bare legs to those horned men hankering for a frolic! Filthy!"

"What was your husband's manner?"

"Oh! Ronald was a strong man of faith. Very strict, and always one to set you right if you strayed from the path. There were times when I had – wavered, and he was there to correct me. It was my fault and I accept his judgement." She softly rubbed the memories on her cheek. "The Lord rest him." Her glossy eyed devotion was almost painful.

Austin was a man of faith, he had to be raised by a priest and all, but he had always tried to keep himself balanced. Sometimes, certain questions in life couldn't always be answered by the good book. No matter how hard he tried.

"Well, thank you ma'am. Might I call on you later if I need to ask you any other questions?"

"Oh, you seem like such a good boy. You go right ahead and stop on by any time and I'll tell you anything you want to know about my husband or that long haired dandy!"

Austin left the devoted widow Svenson to her letter sorting, noticing the shake in her hands that she tried to hide as he left the post office.

Chapter 9

The Donahue

Something about the situation didn't sit right with Austin. From what he's seen and everything he has read in the Marshals 'journal says that Ketchum craves an audience. He needs someone to see him perform and then he feeds from the despair of the one he leaves behind. It seemed odd that he would commit a murder without anyone to witness the heinous act. Then the tell about the musicians was queer with no mention of the husband's suggested affairs as Marshal Boone wrote of. More answers were needed.

Austin located the Donahue. Funny, no matter how small the town is there is always a saloon. It reminded Austin of the one back in Albuquerque that he tried to avoid. A long narrow room with the bar covering nearly the whole left wall, tables of drinking and chance in the middle, paintings decorating the wall opposite the bar, and what appeared to be a small stage set in the very back. The piano was being played badly by some wino who probably believed himself to be just this side Mozart. Most of the patrons were too drunk to care.

There was an open space at the bar that Austin filled. He waited respectfully for a few moments as he stared at the bartender's back before giving a rap on the counter. Austin beheld the largest handlebar mustache he had ever seen waxed into giant curls. He wondered if he could fit his hand through the loops, but resisted the urge to ask. He reckoned the curls wouldn't look so massive if they were on a taller man. The bartender being almost a full head shorter than Austin made the loops seem more like bull horns.

"What can I get'cha?" The bartender asked.

"I want to ask you about the musicians who used to perform here about two months ago."

The bartender cleaned a glass annoyed by the stranger's inquiry. Austin simply continued.

"I hear their was a long haired man with them."

"People here pay for their drinks. If they don't, I ask 'em to leave."

"I don't want a drink."

"They also pay for my conversation."

Austin reluctantly put two bits on the table. The bartender looked at it as if insulted. Austin put down another two bits.

"Did she send you?" The bartender sighed and set down the glass and towel and leaned into Austin's face. "You tell that crazy widow for the last time, I don't know where that long haired dandy went. And, you tell her, that her liquored up husband was never in here the day he left her." He backed away and picked up another glass to clean.

Left her?

The bartender sighed again, "What are you? Some kinda deputy marshal? You workin' for that other one?"

"I'm a bounty hunter. Marshal Boone was shot dead in Albuquerque three weeks ago. I'm following the man who murdered him."

The bartender didn't blink.

"So what do you know about him? He was the leader of the group that played here."

"Ya, and they were good too! I made good business when they were here. They brought in the crowd. Now all I got is some hobo who ain't got a lick of musical talent!" The bartender said loud enough for the piano player to hear.

"Go ta Hell, Smitty!" The wino spat back without turning around or halting his poor playing.

The bartender waived it off.

"I heard something about a woman in the group."

"Lila? Voice of an angel, that one. Why do you think my business was so good? Ronald sure did like her. Came every night and sat right up at the stage. If it wasn't for that loon of a wife, preach'n evey minute of every hour, the man might have had some peace."

Austin tried not to be offended.

"So where does the long haired dandy come along?" Austin asked.

"He doesn't. He was here the whole day with his troupe orchestrating their departure. The man was never out of my sight until they all set out."

Austin was as confused as a blindfolded sheepdog. His face contorted slightly as he tried to make sense of all the stories. He thanked the bartender who tried to set him up with one of the saloon girls before he left. Austin declined and just asked to be told if he learned anything new. The bartender picked up another glass to clean.

∞

It was the first real meal he had eaten in weeks. After putting Jackson up at the livery, Austin used some of the money he had been given by the towns people back home to rent himself a place to stay for the night. The only place he could find was a very small room, or a large closet, that shared a wall with the saloon, making every drunken yelp and tumble an annoyance to keep the sandman away. On the brighter side, the wino's playing seemed to improve. He must have sobered up a bit. It was still taxing as Austin had always been accustomed to the calmness and quiet of the church.

Before retiring for the night, he found a laughing excuse for a restaurant and ate some badly smoked ham and half day old chili. It was enough to fill his belly more than it had been in what seemed like an eternity. The bed was old and misshapen with a collection of curiously colored stains vexing Austin's ability to identify. He laid his own bed roll on top of the mattress, just to be safe. He had thought the noise from the saloon would keep him up all night until he drifted off and snored away to his own satisfaction.

Chapter 10

Old Wounds

A town.
A bartender.
A lady.
A miner.
A young man standing over him...
The widow Svenson.

"Follow her." Said Father Eli.

Austin's eyes snapped open. The images already beginning to fade again. He sat up in bed rubbing out the sleep with his left hand. His eyes fell on the revolver and gun belt that once belonged to the Marshal. It hung on the back of the small chair reminding him of what he once believed to be a righteous cause. He swung out his legs hitting the boots he set beside the bed from the night before. Though the morning sun light peeked through the tiny window which was positioned too high to see out, it allowed the rush of morning air carrying on it the invigorating scent of dampened pine. Better than coffee, Austin felt like a human being again after a real night's sleep and the brisk morning rise.

It was early. Austin wanted to check on Jackson at the make shift livery to make sure he was being treated right. More than all right, Jackson had made some new friends. A mare who had been bunked beside him that he was rubbing snouts with as Austin walked in. As if fearing discovery the two horses turned away from each other immediately upon Austin's entry.

"Am I interrupting anything?" Austin smiled.

Jackson huffed. Austin approached and gently rubbed Jackson on the side of his face as the stud buried his nose softly in Austin's chest.

"How're ya doin' boy? Are they treating you good?"

Jackson was simply happy to see Austin, even with the recent affections of his new girlfriend.

"I'll be back later. Was just checking on ya. You two can get back to business."

Jackson huffed again. Austin smiled and left his trustworthy, if promiscuous, steed to the care of the livery owner and the attractive young mare he had made the acquaintance of. The inhabitants of this small town seemed to be late risers. After three weeks on the road Austin had become accustomed to rising with the dawn. The dreams seemed to make sure of this. Still more images and faces which faded from his clear recollection as he would rub the morning sleep from his eyes. The words of Father Eli always telling him where his next step lay. If he could only figure their meaning. Then from the corner of his eye he saw the widow Svenson skulking behind the wooden structures. She hadn't seen him, but her movements spoke to her own intent of wanting to remain concealed.

Follow her. He remembered.

The widow left the sight of the small mining town working her way between the pine trees having passed over and around three rocky outcroppings. Austin tried his best to keep himself hidden recalling the games of childhood and the care one must take to avoid being found. After the last outcropping, Austin came upon the widow with her back to him standing before a piece of

slightly disturbed earth. He became still to ensure that she did
not hear his approach. Then with sloth like precision he moved
behind the outcropping he passed and removed his hat. When he
peeked around the rocks a moment later, the widow was knelt in
prayer.
Well composed and wrought with grief, the widow gently pulled
a kitchen knife concealed from her billowing sleeve. She grasped
the knife between her hands lifted it to the sky and drove it into
the patch of disturbed soil over and over crying in a fit of passion
and hysteria. Stabbing and stabbing, wailing to the sky, releasing
her ravenous fury onto this small piece of land. Austin lost count
of how many times the knife pierced the earth as he beheld this
spectacle of madness unfold. The widow ceased as quickly as she
began, then wiped the tears from her eyes and the loose bits of
moist soil clinging to the blade. The knife was slipped back into
its 'hiding place and the widow clasped her hands together once
again.

"Thank you Lord." She softly announced her deepest appreciation to the heavens. She stood, turned and with the grace and
elegance of a lady left the site of the disturbed earth, passing the
hidden and petrified Austin whose breath had left him and did not
return until the widow was out of sight and long gone.

He waited until he was certain that the widow was out of sight
and ear shot before leaving his frankly poor hiding place. How
the widow failed to notice him he couldn't figure. Collecting his
courage he moved closer to the disturbed bit of earth marked
clearly by new stab wounds. A sour rank odor became more noticeable as he approached. Fluids drawn to the surface by the
widow's attack brought the nearly unbearable stench to the nose
as fiercely as one might expect.

Austin stood over the patch of poorly leveled dirt. Something
that he learned once was that the length from tips of his fingers
with his arms outstretched was the same as his height. At first
glance the patch of poorly leveled dirt appeared to be about the

same length of Austin's outstretched arms. Austin put on his riding gloves and began to push away some of the loose soil to one side of the stab wounds. As he expected, only a few inches of digging revealed the putrid remains of a badly scarred and rotting face. The remnants of a thick beard remained leading him to the obvious conclusion that this was once a man, and most likely the widow's "missing" husband. Maggots and other creatures of the earth had been feasting on the remains for some weeks now making the face all but unidentifiable save the one unnatural mark of a bladed stab wound directly in the left eye socket. This wound was nowhere near the stabbed earth which would have penetrated the man's chest. It was likely that this was the very wound that had ended his life. Austin buried his nose in his sleeve unable to bear the weight of the stench any longer. He replaced the dirt over the man's face and asked forgiveness for the dead man.

Chapter 11

Truth Be Told

Austin returned to the Donahue which hadn't opened by the early hour that he arrived. Surrounded by a town of late risers was beginning to frustrate him. How can you get anything accomplished if you sleep half the day away? Then he remembered that in Albuquerque the saloon's are always active into the late hours and rarely open before noon. Austin checked his pocket watch. It was almost quarter to eight. He lifted his eyes which fell upon the post office where she was.

Austin was furious. Everything seemed to be spiraling out of control. He was no closer to finding Ketchum and now felt that he had been on a wild goose chase for the past two days with this widow and her claims that Ketchum had been responsible for her husband's disappearance. The only way Austin could think of to get back on the trail was to finish this calamity. Following the journal there was one more person he could speak to. No more playing it nice. Austin set his mind forward and made his way to the Sheriff's office.

∞

"Sheriff? Sheriff!" As Austin knocked on the door to the jail house where the sheriff had his office.

The door unlatched. Sleepy eyed in his forties and still in his long johns the still half drunk Sheriff opened the door with pistol at the ready.

"Who the Hell are you?!" With a touch of Tennessee in his voice.

"Austin Baker. Bounty Hunter."

"And, why in Christ's name are you banging at my door at this hour?!"

"It's nearly eight in the morning. But, you're a month late anyway." Deadpanned face again. Trying not to choke on the thick air of old spirits the Sheriff couldn't conceal.

"Margaret Svenson murdered her husband."

The Sheriff blinked. "What?"

"Get dressed Sheriff. You need to see something."

Austin painfully waited the twenty minutes for the Sheriff to clear his head and get dressed while Austin recounted the events of the morning and a somewhat vague description of how he came by the Marshal's journal. Finally they left the jail house. At almost nine in the morning they arrived at the wounded piece of land where Austin witnessed the widow frantically stabbing the earth.

"Here." Austin pointed to the obvious and dawned his riding gloves to clear away the earth again as the Sheriff stood and watched.

"You say you're a bounty hunter?" The Sheriff asked quizzically.

Austin's heart skipped. "Yes."

"If that's so, why do you care one whip about Ronald Svenson? And, why would you care if Margaret killed him?"

"To serve justice." Austin didn't think, he just responded.

"Justice is often in the eye of the beholder, son. Ronald Svenson was not the saint Margaret makes him out to be."

"Even so. Everyone deserves justice."

"Thought you might say that."

Austin stopped clearing the dirt. His brow scowling as he turned to meet the barrel of the Sheriff's Colt pointed at his head. His eyes widened. No more daisies, he thought. He heard 'Click'. Time stopped.

Nothing happened.

The Sheriff's eyes widened instead. His thumb moved to pull the hammer back for a second try. Austin was already on his feet with the full force of his right fist driving into the Sheriff's jaw, then his left fist, right again. The Sheriff's balance faltered on the large rock behind his feet. The grip on his Colt revolver released. Unable to recover from the pummeling he fell crashing his left side onto the ground.

Austin drew. Eye contact was made.

"Mine is loaded." Austin stated.

"Damn cap and balls!" The Sheriff fumed. Vision blurred. Loose teeth. Pistol out of reach. "If I was twenty years younger..."

"Why?" Austin asked.

"You ain't no bounty hunter!"

"And, you ain't no Sheriff! Why?" Hammer pulled back.

"Oh, I am boy! I protect my own here. Like I said, right and wrong is a matter of opinion. That bastard of a husband beat'n on poor Margaret! Cheat'n on her with that whore of a singer!"

"So you killed him."

"No. Margaret did that. She'd had enough of him and took her good kitchen knife to his eyes, his mouth and the rest of his face. But, do you think that little woman could've carried that big husband of hers all the way out here? That Marshal Boone and his righteous little vendetta against that long haired dandy. That timing was impeccable."

"But you're the Sheriff! You're supposed to uphold the law!"

"Boy, I don't know where you come from, but we make our own justice out here. Margaret is a special woman. She has special needs. This month gone by, I've done nothing but console her to the best o 'my skills. She don't even remember do'n it."

"That's not what I saw --." Then it occurred to Austin. Margaret, not Misses Svenson, not The Widow Svenson, Margaret. The familiar.

"You love her." Austin's tone softened.

He hit the right nerve. The Sheriff cast his eyes down.

"She needs a good man." The Sheriff cracked his voice to respond.

"So the long haired dandy had nothing to do with this."

"No. We just used him. He left town with those musicians. I ain't never seen him since."

Austin was crestfallen.
Austin was relieved.
Austin was furious.
Austin was righteous.
Austin was confused.

"Stand up." Austin ordered.

The Sheriff did.

"Turn away and take five paces."

The Sheriff reluctantly did.

Austin picked up the Sheriff's gun and carried it in his other hand.

"Now what?" The Sheriff asked.

"Back to town."

Chapter 12

Family Loyalty

The return to the small logging town was uneventful and very quiet with Austin keeping four to five paces behind the Sheriff. The two men stopped before they came into full view of the inhabitants.

"You tried to kill me." Austin said finally after almost twenty minutes of silence. The Sheriff stopped and turned back to the young man.

"And, fate spared your life."

"That's beside the point. You pulled the trigger. I should be dead. You are a murderer. Just because you didn't succeed doesn't make you any less of one."

The Sheriff couldn't bare to look into the young mans 'eyes any more. It had all gone too far. The willingness to go to any lengths to protect Margaret, including cold blooded murder had ended any self respect the man had. The Sheriff was never been a great law man, but he'd certainly never been a killer before now.

"You're right." The badge had become to heavy to carry any longer. The Sheriff took it off and dropped it to the ground along with an ocean of tears. Tears of sorrow, tears of relief, tears of fear, and tears of remorse. "I am truly sorry. You got every right to shoot me too. I wouldn't hold it against you neither."

His words weighed on Austin's mind. It was time to decide.

Austin lifted the Sheriff's gun, still in his left hand and with a strong throw of the arm hurled the weapon backwards into the forest. Landing somewhere neither of them could see. Austin looked back into the Sheriff's eyes.

"If I did that, then who would take care of the widow?"

The Sheriff wore his confusion.

"I thought about what you said. How justice is in the eye of the beholder. I left my home to find the long haired dandy. He may not have killed the widow's husband, but he did kill two men right in front of me, one of them I called Father. Then he kidnapped the girl I loved more than anything in the world and left her beaten and raped miles from home. Now she's consumed by hysterics and can't even go outside of her own house. I want the man responsible. All the way here, all I could think about was putting as many bullets through that man's chest as the gun would hold. Then I would reload and do it again. Now... I don't know. But what you did was out of love. Even though one man is dead, and if not for the grace of God, I would have been the second. However, because it was out of fear of losing the woman you care about the most, I can understand. Love can drive you mad. You'll do anything for it. And because I understand... I can forgive you."

Austin holstered his weapon. The Sheriff wiped the river of tears from his face as they heard the sounds of the logging town in full swing with the days' work. Austin took a deep breath and could smell the pine trees once again.

"I don't know who you are, son. But I'll lay odds on you over that long haired dandy. And you may not shake the hand of a man who tried to kill you, but for what it's worth, you've got a friend here."

For a moment, Austin could swear he felt the hand of Father Eli gently resting on his shoulder like he had done whenever Austin was troubled, needed comfort, and especially when Father Eli was proud of him. Austin glanced, half expecting to see an old mans 'hand on his shoulder. His gaze fixed back upon the black eye and swollen lip he had given to the man who was now extending his hand in friendship. Austin stepped forward and extended his own. An unusual bond was formed.

"So where are you bound?" The Sheriff asked.

"I don't know. I've lost two days here looking into business that ain't mine to be putting my nose in. Ketchum is probably long gone now."

"Ketchum? Richard Ketchum?" The Sheriff recalled.

"Yes. How'd you know that? I never mentioned his name."

"Richard Ketchum ain't the long haired dandy. He's a wino who breezes in and out of town. He plays piano over at the Donahue. He has long hair but I've seen him tuck it up in his hat. Never could figure why."

Austin's face went white.

∞

Open for business. The first customers of the day were two men looking for some company from Lilly and Cordelia, four others trying to best each other at poker, the Sheriff with a black eye and a fair shade more sober than usual and one insanely angry young man who claimed to be a bounty hunter.

Austin's hands were shoving the bartender by the lapels of his waist coat up against the back of the bar before he could grab the scatter gun from under the bar to defend himself.

"WHERE IS HE?!" Austin demanded.

"I told you the long haired dandy ain't..."

"RICHARD KETCHUM!! The man playing the piano yesterday!"

"Richard?! I don't fuck'n know! Left outta here when we closed last night."

"Why didn't you tell me?! He was right there! HE WAS RIGHT THERE!!"

"You said you were look'n for the long haired dandy! You never said his name!"

"Well now I'm looking for Richard Ketchum!"

"Did he say where he was heading?" The Sheriff asked.

"What the fuck, Bob?! You on his side? You got some balls come'n at me in my own place!"

"Just answer the question Smitty!" The Sheriff focused every ounce of his newly commanding clarity on to the bartender who traded between the uncommonly sober and somewhat bloodied Sheriff and the bounty hunter's burning fury.

There was no way out of it for the bartender. He delayed his response as long as he dared.

"I asked him where he was going next and he mentioned he was heading to a mining town three days south of here."

Austin released his grip after one last shove into the wall. The bartender attempted to regain his dignity and composure, daggers of rage continued trading between their eyes.

"You ever come in my place again and I will blow a hole in you the size of Texas before you are half way through the door!"

"I don't plan to, you sanctimonious parasite!" Austin all but spitting in his face before turning to the door and departing the Donahue with the Sheriff close behind.

The patrons of the bar collectively sighed. Lilly left the side of the man who she was working.

"What was that, Smitty?"

"Watch the bar, Lilly."

The bartender left the room with his patrons and employees, walked to the back of the saloon and entered the door marked, OFFICE. The door slammed shut behind him. Inside was a desk, a cot and a long haired man changing into a much nicer set of recently laundered clothes than the outfit he was forced to wear the day before. Nicely clean shaven and bathed, humming to himself as he straightened his hat in the mirror hanging on the wall.

"What did you do to that man?!" The bartender asked in the loudest and most forceful whisper he could.

"Did you tell him?" The long haired man asked calmly, as if he was asking what was for supper, while he made the finishing touches bringing every line of his suit to perfection.

Angry, and annoyed at the subject change. "Yes. I told him you are heading to that mining town to the south."

The long haired man smiled to the bartender through his reflection.

"Thank you, Smitty."

"Richard, what did you do to him?" Smitty took a step forward.

"I didn't do anything to him." Replying honestly, turning to face the bartender and look into his eyes.

"Richard, please. This thing that you do, stop. Please."

The long haired man looked back at the bartender puzzled by the very mention of any thing out of order might have been done.

"This thing that I do?" Richard placed his hands on Smitty's shoulders. "You're beginning to sound like Ma."

"There's a reason why she wouldn't speak to you. Even on her death bed."

"I still don't understand why." He really truly didn't.

"Richard... I... I can't... I can't do this anymore. I can't..."

"Smitty! Smitty!" Richard embraced his brother with the deepest level of compassion. Smitty fought between the urges to push him away or hold him tightly in return. He chose the latter and cried into his shoulder.

"Don't worry Smitty. Everything is going to be alright. This needs to be done. Trust in me. You'll understand one day, even if you don't right now. You'll see that what I'm doing is right. You'll see... You'll see..."

Richard absently released his younger brother and returned to the mirror to fix the damage caused by the familial embrace. His humming drowning out Smitty's silent plea.

"Watch him. Let me know when he leaves town." Richard ordered.

Pained, Smitty replied. "Yes, Richard." Turned, collected himself and walked towards the door. Richard Ketchum returned to his reflection and resumed his humming.

"What is that tune?" Smitty turned back and finally asked.

"I don't know. I heard it when I was a boy. Don't remember where. Instruments weren't like anything I'd ever heard, neither. Been trying to piece it together ever since."

Smitty shrugged before returned to his bar and his customers.

∞

Jackson was readied for the next leg of the journey having sadly been parted from his new found filly. Austin had quickly visited the emporium which was happily free of any long line to replenish his supplies. As he finished his preparations he was approached by the Sheriff.

"Mister Baker."

Austin turned to acknowledge his name. He looked into the face of the Sheriff who had taken a moment and done a fair job of cleaning his face.

"Thank you." The Sheriff said. The two men shook hands once again. "Good luck, son."

"You too." Austin placed his foot into the stirrup and mounted his horse. One last look at the man who tried to kill him and became his friend in less than an hour. A gentle tap at Jackson's side and horse and rider were off.

Chapter 13

Stay on the Path

Falling.
Lost.
Running.
Found.

"Stay on the path." Said Father Eli.

Austin's eyes snapped open.

Two days out of Flagstaff and Austin's nerves were still preventing him from getting any good sleep. He could feel those cold eyes watching him. Ten feet away, maybe twelve. That's how close that murdering bastard was and all it would have taken was a glance at his face to see. Games of disguises. Something that Marshal Boone had actually missed in all of his journal entries. Austin wondered how many times Ketchum had been across the room, at the other end of a bar or even sitting inches away and the Marshal never noticed him. Maybe dressed up as a wino, a vagrant, a coal miner, a farmer... anything... everything. Austin would not make the same mistake Marshal Boone made. Dawn had nearly broken over the horizon and it was time to set out. Jackson was awoken and readied for the day of traveling.

Chapter 14

The Nameless Town

Austin and Jackson finally passed a wooden sign marking the entrance to the mining town. 'Welcome to...', the bottom of the sign was missing. It wasn't as easy to find as Austin had thought. The directions of 'three days south' didn't include having to find an unmarked road leading west two miles through some windy hills and steep rocky mountains covered in Austin's new favorite scented tree. The fortunate passing of a wagon exiting the mouth of this hidden pass gave Austin the directions he needed to follow.

Beyond here lie monsters, Austin absently thought to himself. Curiously remembering the tales of sea faring adventurers read to him by Father Eli when he was a boy. Austin rounded a rocky hill along the path and beheld the town below. Jackson stopped in his tracks without a command to do so. If he hadn't, Austin would have made him anyway.

He couldn't reconcile the sudden knot in his stomach or the simultaneous lump in his throat. The oddest feeling of running into an old lover whose memory remains the most passionate in your heart whilst standing before a ferocious grizzly twice the height of a man and howling with tooth and claws ready to strike at the same time. A sudden cascade of terror, excitement, burning curiosity crossed and the intense desire to leave well enough alone. Jackson was equally unsettled. He would not stand still and it took several tugs on the reigns to keep the horse from turning away from the sight of the town.

It's just a mining town. Why do I feel like this?

"Hey. We have to go down there." Austin said to his troubled and intuitive steed, gently rubbing his mane to smooth the worry out of him.

Jackson huffed in protest.

"I know. There's... something. But we need to go down there."

Jackson huffed again.

"Come on." He said before clicking his mouth.

Jackson trotted a little slower than normal as if hoping that Austin would tell him to turn around at any moment, which he would happily oblige. No such luck.

The winding road leveled out into a nearly flat area where the small town was situated north of an opening in the steep semi-rocky hills. The towns people moved about bathed in a cool light reflecting off the vibrant greens of the tall trees. The forest surrounded the town making the whole area appear crisp and serene. Somehow that didn't make Austin or Jackson feel any better.

Austin's mother had acquired a small one room house when Austin was two years old. He never did learn how she got it and was afraid to ask when he got older. Being the only whore in town with a house and a son made her the most well known lady of the night in Albuquerque. After she died, Austin moved in to the back room of the church to be cared for by Father Eli. His old home remained vacant for many years as no one would dare enter it for fear of the consumption that took his mother. At the age of eleven Austin returned to the small house, barely large enough for a bed, a chair and a small pot belly stove. Vague memories and feelings of a tiny room once called home now old and abandoned. Still recalling a sense of returning to a place that held meaning for him.

He found a livery at the edge of town where he could let Jackson rest and maybe find a new mare to court. Jackson was still on edge. He went into the livery looking from side to side as if searching for a means of escape. Austin paid the fare to a tall negro who ran the livery who doubled as the towns 'blacksmith. It was the first time he had seen a negro as the owner and proprietor of any business. Even though the war ended fifteen years ago there was still so much animosity toward the coloreds that seeing one in a position of status was nearly unheard of.

Austin began to wander. Such a far cry from Flagstaff with its 'bitter residence. The people here for the most part seemed happy. They greeted the stranger with genuine smiles. Children played and the sound of laughter bounced from one structure to another. It was such an odd sound now. Austin hadn't laughed in so long he had almost forgotten the last time. He'd been on the road alone for far too long. So driven and so somber. So drained of life now.

The sights of this town were something to behold. The familiar emporium, livery, butcher, baker and undertaker were all on what could be referred to as 'Main Street' along with a barber shop that Austin desperately needed to patronize. Bustling activity of people going about their business without reason to care of Austin's purpose. Strangers must be a common sight, Austin thought. His eyes turned to the end of main street, and then away. He noticed that there was in fact no church just as Marshal Boone's journal had said. His eyes turned to the end of main street, and then away. The buildings were an eclectic combination of exquisite side by side with plain, balancing each other out in a strangely artistic fashion. His eyes turned to the end of main street, and then away.

Austin found himself by a hardware store where he stepped inside to find a young man, no older than sixteen stocking the shelves. Stocky with short brown hair, round cheeks supporting a pair of innocent brown eyes and a physique chiseled by years of heavy lifting. The young man noticed Austin after setting down a pair of commodes on a lower shelf.

"Morning!" The young man said cheerfully. "What can I help you with?"

"Ya, could you help me find the saloon?" Austin replied.

"First time in town?"

"Ya."

"New people in town always have trouble finding Tom's. It's at the end of main street."

Austin wore his befuddled expression for a moment.

"But... I thought this was the end of main street"

The young man couldn't hide his slight smirk as his his gaze shifted to the right.

"Not quite." He said when he returned his attention to Austin. The young man walked Austin back to the front door of the business and pointed to the end of main street. Austin's eyes turned the the end of main street, and then away.

"Look again."

Austin looked right where the young man had been pointing and saw the saloon. The town was constructed beside a nearly sheer rock wall with an opening at the very end of main street. Beyond the opening was more buildings including the saloon that Austin had been looking for.

"That was down right queer.... How often does that happen?"

"Almost every day. Anytime a stranger rides into town."

Absently, Austin thanked the young man and left the hardware store in the direction of Tom's Saloon. The air became heavy as he moved towards the gaping mouth in the hillside married with the oddest sensation of walking upwards on the slight but clearly downwards slope.

He reached the edge of the gaping mouth, standing his ground against the urge to fall on his ass. Beyond the mouth resided the infamous Tom's Saloon to the left. The building itself couldn't have been more than a few years old, yet it appeared to have survived a fire and several other tragedies in it's short life. The tall windmill described by Marshal Boone's Diary spun vigorously in the oddly light breeze. A single entrance facing main street of double saloon doors framed by large windows on either side. The left window bore the name Tom's Saloon in bold and somewhat welcoming lettering painted on the glass. A boardwalk ran the length of the building with a row of windows which looked out from the second floor with a veranda covering the boardwalk itself.

Opposite the saloon were a few more structures including the town bank and the sheriff's office. Then directly ahead at the true end of main street, a beautiful and ornate hotel donning the name Lucy's Landing in a fanciful feminine script on a large sign directly above the doors. Three stories high and dominating the width of the road, Austin imagined that if the president or the king were to stay anywhere, it would be there.

The pit in his stomach returned. The one he felt when he first saw the town from up the road. He positioned one foot behind to balance himself from the dizzying force trying to remove his dignity and push him back. The miners and town's people seemed to take no notice of this as they walked to and fro, in and out of the large rounded intrusion into the hillside. Austin wanted to step forward but was unable to lift the iron weight of his feet. A strong shake to his head to try and clear the nonsense he felt. Closed eyes and a deep breath, followed by all the will power in his heart and strength in his body to take a single step forward.

Nothing.

He had moved no more than two feet forward. The uphill battle had ended as he once again felt level ground. The pit in his stomach had vanished as a cool and comfortable breeze gently caressed his face and ran through his hair and beard. Everything was crisp. The colors of the rock within the surrounding hill face were vivid and clear and so impacting an the eye while birds sung music sweeter than the softest lullaby. Austin felt safe. He felt at home again. Everything was right again.

Austin's attention returned to Tom's Saloon. It was the only place mentioned in the Marshal's journal so it was the first place on his list to visit. Gently pushing open the double doors he felt the circulating breeze from a pair of horizontal windmills attached to the ceiling along with a mechanical contrivance causing them to spin. It must be wonderful in the summer, Austin thought. To the right was the bar of solid oak with miners filling half the stools. Behind it an enormous mirror reflecting the shelves of a vast selection of more varied kinds of liquor than Austin had ever seen. The ceiling was vaulted in the center with a grand staircase leading up to an observation deck looking down on the tables of card games. The faint and familiar sound of working girls satisfying their clients bled from the doors on the upper level. Thankfully it was barely noticeable and easy to ignore over the piano player which Austin made sure to take a good look at before he approached the bar.

After cautiously confirming the identity of the piano player, Austin strolled over to the bar which was manned by a brown haired man in his early forties wearing a neatly groomed beard, a white shirt with sleeve ties on both arms all covering a burly bearish body as evident of his well fed stomach and patch of chest hair poking out from the top of his shirt. The man had a scar on his neck just peeking out from the collar line. It was long and thin, rather like a burn. Austin had seen this kind of scar before on men who fought in the war for southern independence. Those who had been touched by the blistering heat of a rifle ball. Half an inch one way and he would have been dead. Half an inch the other way and he would have never known it was there. Austin presumed that this was Tom, owner and proprietor of the establishment bearing his name. Tom had been watching Austin since he came in.

"Most people come to the bar before they make requests of the pianist." Tom said instead of 'Hello'.

"I needed to make sure." Austin replied.

"Looking for someone?"

Austin was a bit taken aback by Tom's directness.

"Is that any of your concern?" Austin asked.

"This is my place, everything is my concern. My name is Tom... Tom Bell."

"Austin Baker... I'm... a bounty hunter." Barely remembering to squeeze in the last part.

Tom chuckled in disbelief, "Sure you are. What can I get you?"

Austin was dumbstruck. He'd been calling himself a bounty hunter since Flagstaff and he suddenly wondered if his ruse had been transparent this whole time, or if Tom was just that intuitive.

"I-- I'll just have a beer." Austin finally pushed out.

"I have eleven different kinds." Tom replied.

"Try the Guinness." A thick Irish accent said from one of the men sitting at the bar. Austin turned to acknowledge the man who made the suggestion.

"Tom is the only person I know who can get it. I love 'em for it! He still won't tell me how he gets it." The dirty and slightly drunken

Irish miner raised his bottle of dark foamy beer to the bartender.

"He says that every time." Tom said.

"And I mean every word!" The Irishman put his beer into his left hand and extended his right to Austin. "Michael Briody."

"Austin Baker." he replied along with a handshake and the strangest sense of recognition. "Have we met before?" Austin asked.

"Not unless you were in Kildare anytime up to two years ago."

The Irishman was thin but sturdy. Some of the lightest blue eyes Austin had ever seen on anyone staring out from a dirt smudged face which matched his dirt encrusted clothes. Austin was sure that after days of travel and the last bath he took being nearly a week ago that he was no spring flower. But Michael and the other miners at the bar had him beat hands down. Through the filth Austin still couldn't shake the feeling that he had met the Irishman somewhere before.

"No, I've never been out of New Mexico until about a month ago."

"So what brings you here?" Tom asked. Austin turned to Tom and suddenly felt the same recognition as he had with Michael. Seeing him somewhere before but not remembering where.

"I'm looking for someone."

"I gathered that... Bounty Hunter."

"How did you know?" Austin admitted.

"I've met my share of bounty hunters and you ain't one."

"What do I look like then?"

"Like a man running. Running to somewhere, or away?"

"Maybe both." Austin sat down at the barstool beside Michael whose attention returned to his beer and his drinking mates.

"I'd like to ask you something." Austin began. "Do you remember a U.S. Marshal named Boone? His journal says he was here about two months ago."

Tom thought for a moment. "I reckon I do. He was chasing the man who murdered his family. What are you doing with the man's journal?"

"The man he was chasing killed him, in my town, along with the Priest who raised me. After that he kidnapped and raped the woman I love." Some how it didn't hurt as much saying it this time. But the impact was no less intense on the listeners. Michael's attention returned to Austin along with the other miners who overheard.

Austin relayed the details of the story which led him to the bar-stool in Tom's Saloon. By the time he had finished he had the undivided attention of half the room including some of the card players and the Saloon girls. At the end of the story, Tom expertly poured a shot of whisky right up to the edge of the glass without spilling a drop.

"This one is on the house." Tom said as he gently moved the shot forward within Austin's reach. Austin wasn't much of a drinker, but he accepted the offer as the patrons of the Saloon lifted their glasses in respect. Especially Irish Catholic Michael who felt for Austin's loss. Austin took the glass in hand and downed the whis-key in a single gulp, secretly proud of himself that he didn't cough afterwards.

"Can I ask you something else?" Austin said trying to change the subject and keep himself composed.

"Anything you'd like, son."

Austin hesitated for a moment remembering how Father Eli would call him "son".

"How did you come up with the..." He said pointing to the two slowly spinning windmills on the ceiling.

"I didn't. There's a young man in town, 'bout your age, who built it for me. Demanding as Hell and looney as a nut but he can build things you wouldn't believe. Here..." Tom opened an metal box behind the bar and pulled a bottle of beer from it and set it in front of Austin.

"Pick it up."

Austin took the beer in hand. It was cold. Much colder than it rightly should have been. He opened the bottle and took a drink. Austin's expressed his pleasant surprise at how fantastic it was to drink a truly cold beer.

"He introduced me to cold beer just like that." Michael said. "Now the whole town's spoiled. Nothing like it, even in the hot summer the beer is still cold."

"Progress." Tom added. "Cold beer in the hot summer. What's next?" Tom's attention drifted to the window outside. "Must have felt his ears burning. Here comes the whirlwind now."

Austin turned to the doors of the saloon just as he walked in. The cleanest man Austin had ever laid eyes on, even more so than Mister Emerson. Clean shaven, groomed and thoroughly bathed. No more than twenty years old and a couple of inches shorter than Austin, but walking in like he was the tallest man in the room. Intensity with calm and precise control as every step was with purpose and no body movement was random or unplanned. His forehead was donned with the darkest glasses letting so little light through, Austin couldn't imagine what they would be useful for. Thick hyde leather gloves extended nearly up to his elbows covered in what looked like random burn marks. Pressed white shirt and black trousers held up by suspenders just like everyone else and mirrored shine on his boots that had miraculously escaped the dirt from outside.

"Tom!" The man said a full five seconds after stopping just short of the bar.

"Patrick." Tom replied.

"Where's my copper?"

"It's on it's way."

"That's what you said three days ago. How long is this going to take?"

"It takes as long as it takes, Patrick. Have some patience."

Patrick let out a small growl under his breath which was more frustrated with having to wait than confrontational against Tom.

This time it wasn't subtle. A wave crashed against Austin as he looked at Patrick. His face, his mannerisms, his voice. Austin had seen him before. He was absolutely certain of that, but for the life of him he could not remember where or when.

"I know you!" Austin blurted out.

Patrick turned to Austin, locking eyes just made the feeling that much more.

"Um... Okay." Patrick replied.

"I beg your pardon. You all seem so familiar to me. I am sure we've met before."

"Where are you from?" Patrick asked.

"Albuquerque."

"Well, I do get around, but I haven't been to New Mexico... Yet... I think... I'll find out later."

Austin continued to stare, trying so hard to remember. "Beg... Pardon... My mistake."

Austin continued to stare at Patrick, who became nervous but not for reasons Austin would understand.

"Right... No problem... Well... It was nice to meet you...?"

"Au-- Austin. Austin Baker."

"It was nice to meet you Austin." Patrick looked at the bartender. "Um, Tom... Copper?"

"It should be here by tomorrow." Tom replied patronizingly.

"Good." Patrick turned attention back to Austin who hadn't stopped looking at him with the most perplexing stare.

"Okay look, I'm flattered but I haven't... um, turned. Is that the right word?"

"What?" Austin snapped out of it.

"Never mind. I'll see you guys later." Patrick turned with precise movements and left the saloon.

It took several moments for Austin to turn back to Tom and Michael who stood and sat with faces nearly as quizzical as Austin's. Then Tom's eyes narrowed and his head cocked ever so slightly to the side.

"You saw it too."

Austin focused on Tom.

"Saw what?"

"I've been all over this great nation. Done more in my life time than most people have done in ten. I've met men and women from all walks of life. I can size up anyone a mile away, but he is the only person I can't figure. I don't get half the stuff that comes out of his mouth and I don't know where he comes up with it. Sometimes he's funny as hell, other times it's like he ain't all there." Tom said.

"It ain't that. I just... remember him from somewhere. Somewhere important."

"He gave us cold beer!" Michael piped in.

"That he did." Tom agreed. "Son..."

Austin turned back to Tom, the sound of son giving him a slight familiar pinch.

"...You look like you could use a shave, a bath and a good night sleep. The barber shop is just outside the hole. Just tell 'em Tom sent you. Then you come back here and I'll situate you upstairs."

"Thank you Mister Bell."

"Tom. Everyone calls me Tom."

Austin thanked Tom for the whiskey and the advice. He left the Saloon in search of the barber and walked to the point where "The Hole" in the mountain separating the area where Tom's Saloon and the other few buildings from the rest of the town. Austin once again passed the imaginary line, having all but forgotten the forbidding sense he felt when approaching it for the first time. In a single step beyond the edge of the line Austin felt the pressure at his back once again making him now feel a downhill sensation. Austin stopped, gazing over his shoulder at the Saloon he nearly lost his balance from the strange force compelling away. He shook his head and continued to the barber shop.

Tom and Michael continued their conversation after Austin departed.

"So Tom, what do you think about that boyo?" Michael asked, his Irish blood already sobering him up from the alcohol.

"He's honest."

"Didn't he lie about being a manhunter?"

"He lied badly, because he doesn't know how. That means he's used to telling the truth." Tom folded his arms, staring out the doors of his Saloon pondering everything he'd just heard.

"So you think he's tell'n the truth about that Marshal, the Priest and his poor girl back home?"

"Yes, I do."

"So we'd better keep our eyes out for this long haired bastard."

"Yes, we should. I remember him. Hard to miss a fella like that. There was something downright ungodly about about that man. Saw it the moment he breezed in my door like he owned the place."

"What do you think about him knowing Patrick?" Michael gestured to Austin's empty seat.

Tom chuckled. "I don't think Patrick, knows Patrick."

"Amen to that, brother." Michael toasted with the last of his beer.

Tom picked up the shot glass Austin used and washed it with a wet rag he pulled from behind the counter. He looked over to one of his girls who made eye contact and motioned to Michael and back with a silent tip of her head. Tom leaned in closer to Michael after finishing his wipe down of Austin's shot glass.

"So, Michael..." Tom began softly. "When're you gonna pay Lillian a visit? She's been asking about you."

Michael's expression turned sour. Tom knew better. Michael leaned in and matched Tom's quizzical stare with one of extreme irritation.

"I - AM - a MARRIED man Thomas." Michael said as low and forcefully as possible with the most deadpanned expression a half drunken Irishman could.

"That doesn't stop some of your other miners."

As if on cue, Reginald with his missing teeth and overabundance of body hair emerged half dressed from one of the upper rooms with one soiled dove on each arm. Tom looked up and nodded his head. Michael looked up, and then back at Tom.

"The difference is, I LOVE my wife... And my children!"

"But they're still in Ireland."

"Not for much longer. I've almost got enough saved to bring them out here."

"All I'm saying is, how would she know?"

"I would know. And I'd appreciate this be the last we ever talk on the subject. Thank Lillian for her interest, but the answer is still no. And just for that, you can get me another bottle!"

"Yes, sir." Tom backed off and pulled another bottle of beer from the cold box behind the counter.

Chapter 15

Four Bits and a Bed

The statement "Tom sent me" did nothing but produce a cold scowl from Frank Usher, the bitter old barber who didn't blame Austin for Tom's private jab. His skill in grooming was such that most thought he'd been born with a shaving razor in one hand and a pair of scissors in the other. The handles of each fit so perfectly into his aged yet steady hands which had molded over the decades the shape of the instruments. In a ballet of fluid motions, Frank gave Austin the most fantastic shave and haircut he had ever had. Or perhaps it had just been so long since he had one that it just felt that way. In defiance of Tom's Jab, Frank suggested that Austin go to the hotel instead of Tom's Saloon for a good night's rest and a hot bath. God only knows what has gone on in those beds at Tom's, not to mention the fact that Frank didn't owe Tom any favors.

Austin paid for his haircut and shave and decided to take Frank's advice. He walked out of the barber shop clean shaven with the exception of a well shaped mustache. Austin had never worn one before and decided it was time to stop looking like a boy. He pushed through the uphill pressure once again back to the eye of the storm.

The exquisite appearance of Lucy's Landing once again took Austin breath. It seemed so odd to him that a hotel this fine would be found in a dirty mining town when it could stand beside the finest ones in New York and not look out of place. He almost felt unworthy to pass through the doors. The interior of the hotel didn't disappoint. The main lobby was something out of a novel of the high life on the east coast. Crystal chandelier, hand crafted wood accents, a spectacular grand staircase directly ahead of the entrance, an ornate front desk to the right, solid oak set of double doors to the left, crushed velvet on finely detailed furniture and well lit from an array of well arranged lamps which captured the detail and delivered it to the eye in the most pleasing way.

Behind the front desk stood not a woman, but a Lady. Just as refined and elaborate as her hotel. Somewhere in her mid forties, by Austin's reckoning, but she wore her age with beauty and distinction as even the simple task of sorting through the names in the check in book was done with the highest level of grace. He correctly presumed that this was Lucy.

Lucy lifted her eyes which brightened at the sight of Austin, whose face was now well groomed but his clothes desperately needed laundering and a good taylor.

"Welcome to The Landing. May I help you?" Her voice had been crafted by decades of refined authority. Soft and welcoming whilst being strong and unshakeable.

"Good afternoon, ma'am..." Austin removed his hat, timidly holding it with both hands in front of him, shoulders shrinking and voice returning to that of a small boy. "...The barber, Frank, said I should seek lodging here instead Tom's Saloon."

"Of course. Mister Usher is not one to steer you wrong." Lucy replied with absolute precision and clarity in every syllable.

"Mister Usher was very accommodating, and highly skilled at his craft." Austin said.

"You will find many people here are all highly skilled at their craft. How long will you be staying with us?" Lucy asked.

"Forgive me ma'am, but I'm a man of limited means and I fear that a single night here would be enough to take what little I have left."

"Nonsense, young man. If that were true I would not be able to accommodate the large number of people who pass through this town. Also, I never turn out someone into the cold. How does four bits a night sound?"

"That... Sounds wonderful!" He said, shocked at the reasonable price. "That's how much I paid in Flagstaff for a small cold room that shared a wall with the saloon." Feeling more welcome, Austin stepped closer to the front desk.

"I imagine you slept very little that night."

"It was the only real bed I've slept in for a month."

"Then let us remedy that." Lucy replied, checking her available rooms. "I have a room facing the town with a bath and one of my new beds. If you'd like we also have laundry service and I have a taylor nearby who skills match that of Mister Usher as a barber."

"I beg pardon, but how much will that cost?"

"For first time guests, it is a complimentary service."

Austin couldn't believe what he was hearing. "All of that for four bits?"

"Yes, sir." Lucy replied as a matter of fact, continuing her graceful demeanor with every word and breath.

Austin took a deep breath and exhaled with amazement. He pulled the small coin purse from his jacket pocket and pulled four bits to pay for his stay.

"That is not necessary. You can settle up at the end of your stay." Lucy said.

Austin paused for a moment. "I may have to leave in a hurry at some point. I would rather be settled up before hand."

"As you wish. If you'd like I can have someone draw a hot bath for you and we can see to your laundry immediately."

"I am... wearing my laundry, ma'am."

"There are dressing robes in the rooms. Leave your soiled clothes outside the door in the wicker basket provided and they will be tended to."

Lucy tapped the bell on the edge of the counter. A boy of fourteen appeared from a doorway opposite the front desk wearing a bell-hop uniform, clean and pressed as everything else.

"If you will just sign in, sir." Lucy said to Austin as the young bellhop took his place beside the desk awaiting the usual instructions. Austin took quill in hand and signed the check-in book. Lucy then handed the bellhop a set of keys.

"Samuel, will you escort Mister Baker to number sixteen. Have Maryanne draw a hot bath right away and take Mister Baker's clothes to the laundry after he sets them out."

"Yes, Ma'am." Replied the young and energetic Samuel. "Right this way, sir."

Austin thanked Lucy once again. She responded by thanking him in return. The young bellhop led Austin upstairs. Lucy looked back at the check-in book, relieved as she read the name again.

"Austin Baker.... It's about time." Lucy said softly to herself.

Chapter 16

Breakfast

The Town.
The Bartender.
The Lady.
The Miner.
The Young Man standing over him...
Richard Ketchum.

"He's found you!" Father Eli yelled.

Austin's eyes snapped open as his body threw itself out of sleep. If it wasn't for the fact that he was in the most comfortable bed he had ever slept in he may have hurt himself. It took a moment to remember the dark hotel room that he had fallen asleep in. He tried to catch his breath until he realized that he was sitting naked on the hardwood floor several feet away from the bed. The images from his dreams didn't fade this time allowing him to finally remember the dreams that he had weeks before ever seeing this town or the people he had met. Austin's mind continued to race for an hour and half until the sun rose.

Promptly at seven o'clock, as expected, there was a knock at the door and a young lady's voice announcing that his laundry was ready. Having all but forgotten the fact that he was still sitting on the floor without modesty, Austin donned the dressing robe he used while his own clothes were being tended to.

He opened the door to the attractive young lady holding his mended and laundered clothes. The young lady's head shyly cocked to one side as she gingerly explained all of what she did to bring his clothes back to a respectable status.

"You didn't have to go to all the trouble, Miss." Austin replied with a kind smile.

"It was no trouble, Mister Baker." The young lady's cheeks turned a shade redder.

Austin gently took the neatly pressed and folded pile from her hands. The young lady smiled and curtsied slightly before hurrying off down the stairs. Austin smiled again, this time to himself as he closed the door.

It was impressive. The clothes looked better than new. All the stains that Austin had acquired in his journey here had been removed. Tears and holes had been repaired by a master of the craft and everything pressed with starch and pristine. He felt almost unworthy to put his own clothes back on, but that didn't stop him.

∞

"Good morning Mister Baker. Might I say that a good night's rest and bath make you a fair sight for the eyes." Lucy said as Austin presented down the staircase into the active lobby and the sound of dozens of voices behind the double doors across the lobby. Austin looked to Lucy who was behind the front desk where he last saw her. The only thing that proved she hadn't been there all night was yet another elegant dress she wore with her usual dignity and class.

"Thank you Miss..." Austin realized he never learned her last name.

"Misses... Glenn." Lucy replied with her uncommon grace.

"Thank you Misses Glenn. If I might inquire as to a good place for breakfast in this town?"

"Breakfast is included in the cost of your stay. The dining room is through the double doors across the lobby. Today we are serving ham, hash, bacon, sausage, pancakes with syrup and biscuits with hot coffee and tea with lemon. Present your room key to the server so they know you are a guest."

Austin thanked Lucy once again for her gracious hospitality before taking his leave to the dining room.

∞

Austin finally realized where Lucy made most of her money. It looked like half the town was in the large dining room for breakfast. The smell of ham, coffee and pancakes was mesmerizing. Especially to someone who has had little more than fire pit roasted road kill for the better part of a month. Nearly two dozen tables in the room with six chairs at each and all full with a line to the serving counter. Miners who had no where to sit stood with plate in one hand and utensil in other as they shoveled the food into their mouths with the greatest of satisfaction. It didn't seem to matter who you were outside the dining room. Bankers sat beside miners, negro's beside whites and even chinese. 'Everyone is welcome and everyone is equal' said a sign above the serving counter just above the menu and another sign that said, 'Anyone pushing will go to the end of the line!'

How modern. Austin thought.

After ten minutes in line Austin got his ham, hash and biscuits. Fortunately as he was waiting four tables of miners including Michael, the Irish miner he met yesterday, left all at the same time leaving open a number of seats. Michael didn't notice Austin as the miners left for work, bellies full of good food to start out the day. Austin agreed that the ham and hash were delicious but the biscuits did seem a little dry. He didn't care. It was the first real meal he'd eaten in a month. That included the so-called meals he managed to get while he was in Flagstaff. He almost preferred road kill to the slop they served in that town.

After breakfast Austin returned to the livery at the far end of town to check on Jackson. The horse was so happy to see Austin who had been away for what seemed like weeks. Austin could tell that Jackson wasn't very comfortable here. There were three mares in the stable with him and he hadn't made any new friends like he had in Flagstaff. Jackson just wanted to leave. Austin stroked Jackson on his snout to try and comfort him as best he could.

"I know you don't like it here." Austin said. "But he's here. I know he's here. And we've still got a job to do."

Jackson reluctantly huffed in agreement.

Chapter 17

The Young Man

Horse and rider left the livery to explore the local area in and around the town. Together they carefully examined every face they came in contact with. Austin wasn't going to make the same mistake he did in Flagstaff, but that didn't remove the feeling of those cold eyes on the back of his neck he had all day.

Hours of searching and speaking with the town's people did little to present any viable leads. Austin decided to go back to Tom's Saloon to get a drink for himself and let Jackson rest his hooves in front of the horse trough, but Jackson wouldn't have it. He would not cross the point where Austin felt the uphill battle. He went so far as to dismount and tried to pull Jackson in by the reigns. Jackson fought with all his strength which was more than a match for Austin's comparatively gentle pull.

"Goodness, Jackson! It's fine! Look!" Austin passed the threshold and held out his arms beckoning the horse to follow.

Jackson huffed in defiance before slowly turning around and strolled in the direction of the livery.

Austin sighed, but couldn't blame the horse. He caught up with the stud and walked beside him to the livery where he paid Henry Johnson for another night's stay.

"If we don't find anything by tomorrow, we'll leave town and head for the next one in Marshal Boone's journal. Do we have a deal?" Austin said to Jackson.

Jackson didn't huff this time. He just looked at Austin and nudged him with his snout. Something was bothering Jackson, that much was clear. Austin had a little bit of an idea of what he thought it was, but there was no way to tell. Austin stroked Jackson's snout.

"It's alright, boy. I'll be back in the morning."

Austin left the livery, and if horses could cry, Jackson would have.

∞

Austin returned to Tom's Saloon. The upward feeling on the downward slope seemed less pronounced this time. Must be getting used to it, he thought. Austin entered the saloon around one fifteen in the afternoon, walked to the far end of the bar and sat himself on a slightly rickety stool, took a deep breath and sighed more out of exhaustion than frustration. Tom, ever vigilant to his customers, approached Austin, glass in one hand and bottle in the other and always ready to pour.

"How goes your search?" Tom asked.

"Poorly."

Tom poured a shot for Austin, which was not on the house this time. Austin took the small glass and downed it all in a single gulp.

"No one in town has seen hyde nor hair of him and you're the only one who knows what he looks like."

"That's a shame. A bastard like that deserves to be hanged a dozen times for what he's done."

A man with short hair and four day old chops had been sitting by the piano for over an hour attempting to give advice to the man playing who repeatedly told him to "Sod off". He finally relocated to the nearly empty bar three stools down from Austin.

A moment later the whirlwind had returned. Patrick, in his focused chaos walked right up to the bar between Austin an the short haired man, as always drawing the attention to himself. This time dressed more normally with a brown duster and a respectable hat. Both along with the rest of his clothes appearing clean and new.

"Tommm....?"

"Paaaaaatrick...?" Tom replied with a mocking smirk.

"Where's my copper wire?"

"It hasn't arrived yet."

"You said to check with you today."

"Yes I did. I did say to check with me today. It should be here any moment. Would you like a drink while you're waiting?" With his expanding smirk.

Patrick's eyes narrowed and he huffed through his nose in a way that remind Austin of Jackson. Tom looked Patrick square in the eyes holding back a smirk at Patrick's frustration.

"Fine... I'll take a sarsaparilla, and it better be cold!"

Austin didn't know Patrick, but he could tell when someone was demanding for no reason. Austin smiled.

Patrick's finger tapped with a gentle rhythm on the bar, compelling the short haired man beside him to take up humming a tune he had been practicing his whole life.

Austin felt a chill.

Patrick heard the melody being hummed by the stranger beside him. Recognizing it, he began to hum the same tune with the stranger.

The hair on the back of Austin's neck stood up as his heart sank.

The stranger suddenly stopped humming, eyes widening.

"Wait! What?!" Patrick exclaimed, turning to the humming man.

"What?!" Ketchum exclaimed snapping eyes to Patrick.

"WHAT?!" Austin gaze shot beyond Patrick. Those unforgettable cold eyes set in the skull donning a now shortened hair cut.

"Damn! Too soon!" It one fluid motion, Ketchum leapt out of his seat grabbing Patrick with his right arm around his neck and drawing his revolver to Patrick's head.

Austin was slower to the draw. Had it been a dual, he would already have been dead. His own revolver drawn and aimed now.

Tom was last to react, dropping Patrick's sasparilla and reaching for the scatter gun he kept behind the bar for just such an occasion, which sadly seemed to happen more often when he was around than he'd like. He was now drawn on the the two men.

Some patrons took cover, others reached to the concealed pistols they kept which were against the town ordinance, but they had them anyway.

"Whoa! Okaaayyyy!" Patrick replied raising palms to all the people in the saloon with their barrels pointed mostly in his direction. "Would prefer not to get shot today! Would someone tell me what's going on? And, how do you know that song?!"

"How the hell do you know that tune?! You're very calm." Ketchum asked.

"Well... That makes one of us." Patrick replied. The tension from everyone other than himself flooding the room.

"Why?" Austin asked boldly, barrel trained but without skill to trust the shot to the intended target.

"Why what?" Ketchum replied.

"YOU KNOW DAMN WELL, WHAT!! Father Eli! Marshal Boone! His family! ... ABIGAIL ... and Lord knows how many others!!"

"What did he do to them?" Patrick asked.

"He murdered some, raped others, and in some cases both!"

"Eww, Stop touching me!" Patrick said.

"ANSWER ME!!" The command in Austin's voice could no longer be disobeyed. He peered into Ketchum's eyes, no longer afraid of the man who took everything away from him.

"Love." Ketchum finally replied with cold sincerity.

"What?!" Austin replied. "Are you saying you loved them?!"

"No. You loved them. Marshal Boone loved his family, and you loved yours. I cannot allow that."

He meant every word.

"What?!" Patrick asked. "Seriously?! That is the stupidest thing I have ever heard! Wait! Don't tell me... You were robbed of your love when you were younger and now you are punishing the world for it, or something ridiculous like that, right? ... People die. Even the ones we love. When it happens It hurts... worse than anything... It tears out your heart replaces it with a black lump of coal forever, and anyone who says otherwise is lying. But we have to move forward. It's shitty, believe me I know! If you're lucky you have something crazy enough come along to take your mind off of it for a while. But it never really heals and the people you lost are never really far from your mind even though you act like they are for everyone else's benefit. In the end it just leaves scars that you have to live with."

Spoke the voice of experience. Everyone listened, except one.

"I disagree." Ketchum said smoothly. "If God... or one of his servants, is responsible for taking the love of your life away from you..." Ketchum looked Austin square in the eyes. "...Then you should punish God and his servants for committing murder." it was a statement, not a question. "The commandments of God state, Thou Shalt Not Kill. Should not God be held accountable to his own laws? And God is love."

Austin could not help but think of Marshal Boone. He knew exactly how the man was feeling. The soulless outlaw holding a man hostage to ward off the retaliation of those holding pistol in hand and fingers itching to squeeze. There was a profound moment of silence. A realization that everyone felt, but only Patrick could put in to audible clarity.

"Okay.... You are fucking nuts."

Patrick could hear the sound of Ketchum grinding his teeth behind his right ear, tightening his grip around the young man's neck. His eyes burned. His purpose set aside to answer a deeper question.

"How do you know my song?" Ketchum demanded.

"Your song?" Patrick replied. "That sure as hell ain't your song!"

"How do you know that?!"

"Because, number one, it is impossible for you to even know that song, and number two, you were only humming the lyrics, not the actual tune."

Ketchum's eyes became wider, if that was even possible.

"Um, Patrick. Have you finished?" Tom asked, shotgun still aimed true.

"Oh... Sure." Patrick replied ever so casually before moving even faster that Ketchum did. A hit of the hand holding the revolver at the moment a powerful elbow drove into the outlaw's gut. The gun fired into the air, bullet missing Patrick's head by mere inches, but it was enough. Freed to move, a blur of punches and kicks removing Ketchum's focus.

An opening.

Tom and Austin took aim.

Tom fired, Austin didn't.

Tom missed... almost.

The slurry of pellets whizzed between Patrick and Ketchum, two pellets grazing the outlaw's arm. The smoke from the black powder clouding their vision and rang their ears.

"JESUS CHRIST, TOM!!" Patrick yelled over the high pitched whine now deafening his ears.

Ketchum didn't wait to see if he was injured. Bolting for the door as a small hail of bullets from some of the patrons also failed to reach their target.

Austin saw Ketchum leap through the saloon doors and wasted no time in channeling all of his rage into power for his legs.

"EVERYONE STAY HERE!" Patrick shouted as he also shot out the doors in pursuit, mustering what he could to keep his balance while the whole world whistled.

Ketchum was heading towards the mouth. A group of miners including Michael blocked the path. Without thinking Ketchum turned and headed behind the buildings opposite the saloon. Austin and Patrick gave it their all to follow Ketchum.

He won't get away this time! I won't let him! Thought Austin.

Some trees and brush obscured the rock wall that the outlaw had forgotten about and was fast approaching. Austin holstered his gun. There was no way to get a clean shot.

Run! Catch him! He knows something! Thought Patrick.

Patrick didn't see the fallen tree branch until it was too late. At full speed he threw his foot into it and planted himself on the ground a moment later. Austin didn't stop, He didn't even notice that Patrick was right behind him. All he could see was the back of Ketchum's head getting closer.

Ketchum's decision to run through the buildings and trees came to bite him. The solid sheer rock wall appeared before him and extended in both directions rounding back to the mouth. He stopped himself just short of ramming it. Turned around in time to see Austin leaping into his chest.

Ketchum landed hard on the concrete floor of the alley way with Austin's weight driving him into it. The cool humid air from Lake Michigan blew through the alley like a wind tunnel. The putrid smell of piss and rotten food emanating from a nearby dumpster. It was morning. Distant sounds of train wheels on rails echoed from the distance while Austin drove fist after fist into Ketchum's face.

Patrick recovered from his stumble and raced to the edge of the rock wall where he found the two men absent, but felt the cool sea air and could smell that wretched filthy dumpster he hated so much.

"Oh... SHIT!!" Patrick exclaimed before hastily walking through the solid rock wall.

It took eight rage driven impacts of his knuckles before Austin was able to take notice of his surroundings. Bloodied, bruised and with two loose teeth, Ketchum returned the favor with a semi hard hit to Austin's jaw. Austin lost the upper hand as Ketchum knocked him to his side and put Austin on the receiving end of a few clumsy knocks. Hands grabbed the outlaw and threw him off causing Ketchum to roll a few times before coming to a stop. Austin looked up and saw the image in the dream of the young man standing over him, and remembered.

"Are you alright?!" Patrick asked, extending his hand.

It took Austin a moment to collect himself.

"Come on, get up!" Patrick said.

Austin took Patrick's hand and was pulled to his feet, as Ketchum drew his revolver again. Patrick yanked Austin behind the foul dumpster as three bullets were deflected off of the thick metal. Confused, Ketchum ran from the alley onto the side walk.

Patrick peeked around the dumpster just in time to see which direction Ketchum went.

"We gotta get after him." His attempt to stand was halted by Austin's grasp firmly pulling him down to meet his most serious gaze to date.

"WHAT THE HELL HAPPENED?! WHERE IN THE HELL ARE WE?!!"

Patrick looked Austin in the eyes, gently placed his hands on the ones holding him by the collar and returned his own look of absolute seriousness.

"South Chicago, Illinois. It's the year Nineteen Twenty-Seven."

Austin blinked.

Chapter 18

South Chicago, Illinois. Fall 1927

For the first time since he could remember, Richard Ketchum was lost. Too much had happened too fast, even for him and he simply couldn't keep up. His mind raced with the thoughts of being so wounded, the young man named Patrick who knew his song, note for note, and the buildings surrounding him. At first glance it was no more than a quiet row of familiar styled houses on one side and tall brick and masonry buildings beside the alley he had emerged from. Through his blurred and beaten vision he beheld an object approaching on the smooth road. A long shiny metal box like a train car, but with small black wheels and making the sound of a choking steam engine. No horse drew it forward. Instead it was it's own self propelled carriage with men and women sitting inside surrounded by wide panes of glass. The wheeled metal self propelled train car coasted by, the riders casting their eyes at him, mouths open and faces a gasp.

Ketchum stumbled forward as quickly as he could. He didn't know where he was or how he got there, but that would have to wait. Austin Baker and his new dangerous friend were close behind. Ketchum found a pair of large wooden doors on one of the brick buildings he was passing. He looked back to see the two men emerging from the alley, more cautiously giving chase. Ketchum made a decision and entered the double doors and discovered that they lead into a church. Another church. This time it was bit more crowded.

Ketchum didn't waste time. He ran quickly up the isle past the well dressed Italians straight to the aging priest giving sunday sermons. It was time to take a hostage again. Ketchum's favorite part. The rush of the moment. This was so much greater than anything he had ever experienced before. Ride it out. Stretch it to it's end and savor every moment. Ketchum caught eyes with the old preacher who returned his gaze with silent disgust.

Patrick and Austin entered the church moments later to see the bloodied outlaw holding the old priest hostage, pistol drawn and held to the aging man's head. Austin beheld the sight once again. All the emotions flooding back into him. Austin drew his pistol and held fast.

"Wait a minute, weren't we just here?" Patrick asked.

"Yes. We were." Austin answered, but not to Patrick. "This is how it all started."

"No, but seriously, A hostage again? Is this all you do? What kind of a bad guy are you?" Patrick mocked.

"SHUT IT!"   Ketchum shouted.   "SHUT YOUR GODDAMN MOUTH!!"

"Watch your language, young man..." The Priest said very calmly. "This is a house of God."

"ENOUGH!" Ketchum cried out. He had lost control of the situation. A very rare thing for him.

"You will answer my questions now!" Ketchum yelled at Patrick.

"Oh come on, do I have to? Can't you just go quietly?" Patrick replied in the most annoyingly sarcastic tone he could muster. Ketchum pressed the barrel of his revolver harder on the priest's head.

"Okay, Okay. Fine. Ask away." Patrick folded his arms, more annoyed than angry.

"How do you know my song?"

"I already told you, it's not your song. You can't have come up with that tune because the melody you were humming was only the lyrics. It wasn't the actual music.... Wait. You're not freaked out by where we are or how we got here? Why aren't you asking about that?"

"How can you possibly know my song?!"

Patrick was struggling to understand how or why the outlaw was more concerned about a piece of music rather than deal with the situation at hand.

"Are you trapped in your own head or something? Seriously, no one is this sociopathic." Patrick said aloud but more to himself than any one who might be listening.

"NO!! TELL ME!! TELL ME NOW!!"

It was the strangest sensation Austin had to date. He had built up Richard Ketchum as a devilish monster capable of horrible evils. This was all still true, but Austin suddenly had a complex epiphany. The mistake Marshal Boone had made was that he always allowed Ketchum to control the situation, and until now Austin had done the same. Things weren't going the way Ketchum had planned or expected so he couldn't adapt to the looney things happening around him. His mind had closed completely to his environment. He was trapped in this situation. Was he always like this? Patrick told Austin that this was Chicago and it was the year nineteen hundred and twenty-seven. An important detail needing further explanation, but it could wait until later. Ketchum didn't seem to understand that. He wanted control again. He needed control again. He needed his performance to be the way he imagined it. Then it all became clear. Richard Ketchum was nothing but a child who wasn't getting his way. For the briefest moment, Austin almost felt sorry for the man. Then it passed with his new found understanding.

"Don't tell him." Austin said with smooth intent.

Patrick looked to Austin questioningly.

"You haven't been playing by the rules." Austin said.

"What? Is this all a game?!" Patrick asked.

"Not a game, a script." Austin motioned with his pistol at the childish outlaw. "His script, and you aren't playing in character."

The expression on Patrick's face shifted from confusion to understanding.

"I will kill him if you don't tell me, I swear!" Ketchum demanded with all the intensity of a child threatening to hold their breath.

"Wow... You really are a one dimensional villain, aren't you?" Patrick replied.

"Are you just going to stand there and talk him to death?" One of the well dressed Italians in the front row asked very politely.

Patrick had all but ignored the people in the church who he just realized were much more composed and better dressed than most church goers should have been. Especially in this situation. The well dressed man who spoke had a thick face, pale skin and wore his hair slicked back with noticeable scars on his cheeks.

Patrick blinked.

"Oh..." He quickly glanced at the other men who all stood with their eyes on the outlaw holding the priest. All with one hand holding their jackets slightly open with the other reaching inside firmly gripping something with anticipation.

"Ohhhh.... I am very, very sorry we disturbed all of you. It was not our intention. We were just chasing the crazy guy who is holding the priest right now. He ran in here, we are trying stop him."

"Are you coppers?"

"No sir. Certainly not dressed like this. Like I said, we were just chasing the looney guy."

"He killed my Father and then raped and beat the woman I love." Austin quickly and cleverly threw in.

The scar faced man turned to the outlaw. "You'll want to let go of Father Eli now."

Austin's ears perked up and his heart sank. It wasn't the same man, but the name was enough.

"NO! NO! NO! TELL ME NOW!!" Ketchum said still focused on Patrick.

Patrick stood for a moment glaring at the outlaw. He turned to Austin who he could tell had regained a level of composure he had been lacking until now.

"Now... Give him what he wants." Austin said coldly.

   Patrick sighed, "Okay, Fine..." cleared his throat, took a step forward and began to sing "Richard Ketchum's" song, mostly on key.

"Sweet dreams are made of this
Who am I to disagree?
I travel the world
And the seven seas,
Everybody is looking for something.
Some of them want to use you
Some of them want to get used by you
Some of them want to abuse you
Some of them want to be abused."

Tears welled in Ketchum's eyes. The scar faced man and some of the more emboldened church goers clapped lightly.

"Thank you!" Patrick smiled. "Wow, that song is actually kind of appropriate right now, isn't it?"

"...How...?"

"That song is older than I am." Patrick snorted.

"It's MY SONG... I heard it in a dream when I was a boy. I've been perfecting it my whole life! I've written symphonies based on that song!"

"You wrote symphonies based on a song from the eighties? ...Dude, really? No wait... Really?!"

"It's time." The old priest said quietly.

Richard Ketchum received another elbow to the nose, forcing the outlaw to lose his grip. The priest swung around and clocked Ketchum in the nose. This was just too much for his already beaten face to take. The gun fell when his orientation was lost. The well dressed Italians produced an array of pistols from their jackets and all took aim as did Austin. Ketchum shoved the priest to the ground and turned to run, unable to grab his gun as he tried to escape.

"NO!" The Priest commanded. "DO NOT SHOOT HIM!"

The urge to do so, even in a church was almost too much to resist.

The aging but still feisty priest stood up as Ketchum ran out a fire exit to the side of the pulpit.

"DON'T LET HIM GO! NOT AGAIN!!" Austin yelled.

Ketchum burst through the door into the alley beside the church, grabbed the door and slammed it hard against Austin and Patrick just as they were about to rush out. It slowed them down just enough to give Ketchum a moment head start. The duo regained their senses and followed out the door giving chase yet again. Richard Ketchum emerged from the alley way into the street.

He didn't see the bus coming.

His body absorbed all the force from the flat front surface of the vehicle at thirty miles per hour. The bus driver slammed the breaks shaving rubber from the tires onto the street. It took fifty-seven feet for the bus driver to stop the vehicle after Ketchum's body was hurled to the side and impacted seven times on the concrete sidewalk.

Austin and Patrick stood dumbstruck.

Witnesses gasped and chirped screams. Some turned away in horror of the spectacle while others couldn't. Austin absently holstered his pistol as his feet carried him gingerly to the outlaw's broken body. There was no more twisted smile from his perverse face. There weren't even enough teeth left to make a smile. Every part of his body was broken with the exception of the man's frozen eyes. He never suffered. He never felt the guilt for his actions nor the punishment customary for those convicted of such deeds. Austin stood over the body of Richard Ketchum. The monster. The Beast. The definition of evil as Austin had known it. The man who had taken Austin's life away and then let him live to experience Hell itself.

The burden lifted from Austin's soul. In a single swift moment the Lord's justice had been done, and Austin had been spared.

It took a full two minutes of the spectators watching before the bus driver and passengers moved to the aid of the outlaw's lifeless body. Someone dashed into the church to use the telephone and call for the police. The well dressed Italians gathered behind the two frontier cowboys. Patrick could only muster the weakest of snide comments.

"Well... Shit."

Chapter 19

Why He Lied

The police had finally come and spoke with the bus driver and then heard the story from the people in the church. Patrick pleaded to the scar faced Italian asking him not to mention the two of them. Once the police saw the scar faced Italian, they didn't ask too many more questions. Before the police arrived Patrick and Austin found a fire escape and climbed to the roof of one of the nearby buildings to wait. Austin occasionally peered over the edge to watch the crowd, the police, and the coroner take Richard Ketchum's body away.

"What would have honestly done if you had caught him?" Patrick asked.

"I intended to take him to jail. Even after everything he did, I wanted him to stand before a jury and face the law. Face Justice." Austin replied honestly.

"Funny how that is. Karma has a way of working out justice on it's own without any help." Patrick replied.

"The Lord works in mysterious ways." Austin said, expecting to gauge what Patrick's response would tell him about this man.

"I'm... not religious. I believe in science. I believe in what can be proven with evidence. Never really felt the need to whisper into the sky and ask for help. It never seemed to work for me anyway."

"But you just spoke of Karma. So you do believe in something more than just what you can see."

"I guess I did. Maybe. I'm not sure."

"I suppose that's a start.... So... ?"

Patrick knew what was coming next.

"So...." Patrick began. "I think the first thing I should ask is, can I trust you?"

"Can *you* trust *me*?" Austin replied.

"Well, this situation is very unusual, but you handled yourself pretty well in there."

"As did you." Austin replied, looking out onto the Chicago sky-line.

"Thanks." Patrick followed Austin's gaze to the city of Chicago. Taking in the sights and absorbing the beauty of it. It's something he never really did before. He would ignore a beautiful day, blooming flowers, and sunsets. Everything was always just there to Patrick. Never beautiful, but never ugly.

"So....?" Austin said again.

"So.... I don't have all the answers yet. As near as I've been able to figure out, part of the town has been built inside of a bubble in time. It's like a hub, or the center of a wheel where all the spokes converge. When you walk off in different directions and pass through the edge of the bubble it instantly takes you to different times and places in history. Then, to return home all we have to do is pass through the space where we came from at a precise angle and then we are back in the old west... I mean the town. There are thirty-six openings around the perimeter of the bubble that go everywhere from ancient rome, all the way to the end of the twenty-first century. But the bubble itself is physically in the year eighteen-eighty. I found it almost a year ago. Long story how, and I've been trying to find out how and why it's even there in the first place."

Patrick paused for some time allowing Austin a moment to absorb what he had been told.

"I'll be honest..." Patrick finally continued. "It's been hard keeping this all to myself. It would be nice to be able to talk to someone who understands without having to edit myself all the time. I forget sometimes and stuff just slips out. I have to be more careful. Historical events that haven't happened for you yet. Terms and knowledge that haven't been discovered. Not to mention just the way people act and behave in different eras. And I've been trying to find answers and doing it all alone."

"Is that an invitation?"

"Maybe."

"What have you learned?"

"So far, not much. I've only been through a few of the holes and I haven't run across anything that might shed some light."

Austin took a deep breath, trying to take it all in.

"Does anyone else in town know?"

"No. At least I hope not, and I'd like to keep it that way. I've had to maneuver greedy prospectors and so-called entrepreneurs away without them noticing. If some selfish idiot were to find out about the town's secret, there is no telling how much damage they would do all for the pursuit of money."

"So... then, where are you from?"

"Where I'm from is Phoenix, Arizona."

"Phoenix? I've never heard of it."

"It becomes the capital after Arizona became a state."

"Became a state? Then, what year do you call home?"

"I was born in the year nineteen-ninety two. For me, it's near the end of the year two-thousand fifteen."

It took Austin a moment to form the next question.

"And, Ketchum's... 'song', that he was so obsessed with..."

"...doesn't come out until the nineteen-eighties." Patrick finished

"It's from the future?" Austin realized.

"Now do you understand why I told him that he couldn't know that song."

"Of course, but then how did he?"

"I don't know. That's just one more mystery to add to the couple hundred that I'm trying to solve about the town. But, I lost a puzzle piece today. I've been desperately searching to find something to help me figure this all out, and when it finally shows up, it ended up being a crazy dude who got hit by a bus."

"Do you think he was from the future too?"

"I don't think so. If he was he wouldn't have been so obsessed about that being *his* song. But some how he heard it and held onto it. Now this is the weird part. That was... one of my favorite songs when I was a kid. I listened it a thousand times growing up."

"Really?"

"Okay, maybe not really a thousand. One thing you'll have to learn is that people from the future exaggerate a lot."

"People from the present exaggerate a lot." Austin replied plainly.

Patrick smiled, "True." Patrick chuckled. "But this takes getting a tune stuck in your head to a whole new level."

Austin smiled. He actually, really smiled. He was spared the need to take a man's life, even a vile one such as Richard Ketchum. Austin looked down to see a long black horseless carriage with it's large doors on back closed with Ketchum's body inside. The carriage, clearly some future hearse, made an sound awful to Austin's ears as its 'engine roared to life and propelled itself away.

"What's going to happen to him?" Austin asked.

"No identification. No relatives to claim him. Testimony from one of the biggest mob bosses in Chicago. He's going to be buried in some random cemetery with no headstone and no one to mourn for him."

"Forgotten?"

"Most likely."

Austin watched the black coroners truck drive off down the street and turn a corner.

Richard Ketchum was gone, and so was the weight on Austin's heart. Justice was done. Not by his hand, but by the hand of God as Austin saw it.

Chapter 20

Homeward

Austin and Patrick returned to the alley where they had emerged. The events still racing through both of their minds as it was time to return home. The two young men stared at a blank wall near the large metal garbage dumpster they had took cover behind a couple of hours earlier. The bullet dents reminding them how the metal dumpster saved their lives.

"My biggest fear is that one day they are going to put that dumpster in the way of the hole and I'm going to be unpleasantly surprised." Patrick said in a half sarcastic tone.

"How is this done?" Austin asked.

"Well look." Patrick went up and put his hand on the wall where the hole was, then he smacked his lips, always half disgusted. "Ugh... Bandaids and ozone!"

"What was that?" Austin asked.

"The doorways all taste different."

Austin was back to a quizzical expression.

"I'll explain later." Then Patrick knocked the wall with his knuckle.

"You can touch the wall and nothing will happen, but if you walk straight at it, it will take you through. There's also this mental component. You have to know it's there and want to pass through it. But that only works when you are on this side of the hole. That's why you were able to pass through it from the bubble side without knowing about it."

"So we have to walk into the brick wall?" Austin said, dubious to the end result.

"Here." Patrick took hold of Austin's arm just above the elbow.

"Close your eyes." Patrick said.

Austin scowled.

"Trust me."

Austin trusted him and closed his eyes, already knowing what was next.

"Now... Walk."

Without sight, Austin took five steps forward and stopped when Patrick pulled on his arm.

"Open your eyes." Patrick said.

Surrounding Austin were trees, the smell of pine, a solid rock wall behind him and the structures of the small mining town not far away.

"I didn't feel anything."

"See, nothing to it."

Austin smiled again, facing this new reality with wonder and curiosity. The two men began walking back to town. Austin glancing back at the rock wall they just emerged from. He shook his head and took in the deepest breath of that wonderful damp pine.

"What are you going to do now?" Patrick asked.

"What do you mean?"

"Are you going to go back to Albuquerque?"

Austin had actually allowed other thoughts to occupy his mind. In the weeks he had been gone, Albuquerque had become a hazy memory from another lifetime. Abigail, would she see him again? Could he go back there? Was there anything to go back to? How could he build a new life there after all of...

The quiet forest air suddenly ripped open. The burst of a nearby explosion caught both of their attention. The shock penetrated their eardrums while the rumble could be felt in the earth below. Moments later, the hazard bell rang loud and hard. Cries of pain and terror and calls for help quickly followed.

"I think that came from the mine." Patrick announced.

Without exchanging a glance, the two men were off in a shot.

Epilogue

The Music

There were one hundred and forty seven electrodes connected to the young boys brain. His neural pathways sparked and fired under all the connections. While the tech was seen as outdated in most circles, the pathways were aligned nicely for the task at hand. Seventy two percent and climbing. A vivisection had been performed to observe the reactions to the internal organs with care to keep the subject alive and viable for study. The methods used were nothing new yet some improvisation had been required to adapt the local instruments to their current purpose. The myriad of proceedings were being observed by a legion of monitors and regulators to prevent things from going south at this critical stage.

Somewhere in the distance an infant wailed. The sharp cries echoing like needles dragging on glass.

A tall man clad in a white surgical gown sighed and moved from behind an observation window. He moved with wide steps through a side entrance and up a narrow staircase to the adjoining upper rooms of the laboratory. The boy on the table slowly clawed his way back into consciousness as the low calming words of the scientist upstairs put the child's complaints to rest.

One eye slowly opened, then the other. A few weak rasping

breaths pulled him back into the room. Unusual steel and chrome instruments surrounded the young man as his reeling mind struggled to make sense of the scene around him. Numbness and a heavy blanket of fading sedation marred his senses but as his vision cleared the image of his own chest opened to the air held by metal clamps snapped the boy back to reality. Wires and tubes spanned his small body. Thin metal rods were driven into his skull like horrific antennas while shrill, unnerving noises came from Lovecraftian boxes lining a series of tables. Try as he might the boy could not move even as his mind screamed in sheer terror his lips were silent.

The most unusual music began to resonate from the room upstairs. Muffled and foreign as it penetrated the ceiling. The child above had gone quiet. Somewhere a door quietly opened and shut.

The clacking of dress shoes rung out on the stairs as the scientist returned to the lab.

The man in white loomed over the young boy. Hot tears burned down the boys cheeks as he gazed into the man's eyes pleading with him to explain why he had awoken to this hellish situation. "Ah.. I see you have regained your senses." The Man slowly grinned, his face lit with elation. "Good. Now we can truly begin. Richard, is it?"

Finally, a scream escaped Richards lips.

Afterword

Next Book:
Secrets

I would like to thank all of you who chose to read this book. My first endeavor at publishing a story I've had running in my head for over twenty years.

www.ingramcontent.com/pod-product-compliance
Lightning Source LLC
Chambersburg PA
CBHW031258130726
47988CB00007B/2636